Meena

MEETS
HER MATCH

meena
MEETS
HER MATCH

By Karla Manternach

Illustrated by Rayner Alencar

Simon & Schuster Books for Young Readers
New York   London   Toronto   Sydney   New Delhi

SIMON & SCHUSTER BOOKS FOR YOUNG READERS
An imprint of Simon & Schuster Children's Publishing Division
1230 Avenue of the Americas, New York, New York 10020

SIMON & SCHUSTER BOOKS FOR YOUNG READERS
is a trademark of Simon & Schuster, Inc.
For information about special discounts for bulk purchases, please contact Simon & Schuster
Special Sales at 1-866-506-1949 or business@simonandschuster.com.
The Simon & Schuster Speakers Bureau can bring authors to your live event. For more
information or to book an event, contact the Simon & Schuster Speakers Bureau
at 1-866-248-3049 or visit our website at www.simonspeakers.com.
Book design by Tom Daly
The text for this book was set in Excelsior LT.
The illustrations for this book were rendered digitally.
Manufactured in the United States of America
1218 FFG
First Edition
2 4 6 8 10 9 7 5 3 1
Library of Congress Cataloging-in-Publication Data
Names: Manternach, Karla, author.
Title: Meena meets her match / Karla Manternach.
Description: First edition. | New York : Simon & Schuster Books for Young Readers, [2019] |
Summary: "Third-grader Meena Zee navigates the triumphs and challenges of family,
friendship, and school while being diagnosed with epilepsy"—Provided by publisher.
Identifiers: LCCN 2018007363 | ISBN 9781534428171 (hardcover : alk. paper)
| ISBN 9781534428195 (eBook)
Subjects: | CYAC: Friendship—Fiction. | Family life—Fiction. |
Schools—Fiction. | Epilepsy—Fiction.
Classification: LCC PZ7.1.M368 Mee 2019 | DDC [Fic]—dc23
LC record available at https://lccn.loc.gov/2018007363

*To Amelia and Mara—for you,
and because of you*

1

I circle my arm around my President Portrait so nobody can see it.

In the picture, I'm wearing a fancy suit that's red, white, and blue. I'm holding a great big cake with squiggly frosting. Here's what it says at the bottom:

> *If I were president, I'd hire a whole team of chefs to bake cakes for me to decorate. They'd make all different flavors of frosting, except for cream cheese, and they'd never try to sneak bananas into the batter to cut back on added sugar, because these people are professionals.*

I peek at the other pictures in our pod. Last time Mrs. D rearranged the room, she put our desks in groups of four, facing one another. My cousin Eli sits on my left. He's been into nature since we were little, so I'm not surprised to see that if he were president, he'd go around planting trees. Our friend Pedro sits on my right. It turns out if he were president, he'd hang a basketball hoop on the Washington Monument so all the tourists could play.

Huh. I forgot the president is supposed to do things for other people.

I glance at Sofía's picture on the desk across from mine. When Mrs. D picked our new spots, she didn't know we don't sit together anymore—not if we can help it. Even though Sofía's picture looks upside down from here, I can still see stars shining through a night sky on her paper. She's drawn a bunch of people stretched out on blankets in the

grass with roses all around them. Here's what hers says at the bottom:

If I were president, I would invite all the fighting countries to the White House for a sleepover. We'd camp out in the Rose Garden, only instead of sleeping, we'd stay up all night talking. In the morning everyone would be friends and there would be peace on earth.

Okay, I can't actually read upside down. I just happened to see it when Sofía went to sharpen her pencil and I turned her paper around.

"Mrs. D?" I ask, waving my hand in the air. "What's the prize if you win?"

"It's not a contest, Meena."

"But let's just say your portrait turns out to be the best one in the class," I say. "What do you get?"

"You don't get anything. I just want you to do your best work." Mrs. D looks around the classroom. "Does everybody understand that?"

When Sofía nods, her poufy flower headband bobs up and down. It's red today and makes her look like a birthday present.

I tap my pencil against the paper. I don't care that it isn't a contest. I want my portrait to be the best one in the class. Mrs. D is hanging these up in the hallway for Presidents' Day in a couple of weeks, and everybody will see them!

Maybe I'd better squeeze "peace on earth" in there somewhere.

I add a couple of more lines at the bottom:

Also, I'd have the chefs bake enough cupcakes to share with the whole world. I'd add rainbow sprinkles to every single one, because there can never be peace on earth until we stop fighting over who gets the sprinkles.

There! My portrait is almost perfect now. I just need to color in President Meena's face and hair.

I wish I were made up of better colors in real life. When I used to draw pictures of Sofía, I could use the brown crayon for her skin, but I have to use that peachy-blah one for mine. I got to color practically anything I wanted for Sofía's eyes, too, because they're this greenish, brownish gold. Every time she wears a different headband, her eyes change—like those rings we got at the carnival that turned different colors when we breathed on them.

I sigh and start coloring the eyes in my por-trait. I make a few dots of light blue, a few dots of

How did *that* happen?

Everyone watches Mrs. D come back over and pick up my paper. I feel the front of my neck get hot. Even Sofía has a worried crinkle between her eyebrows, as if she cared—as if she's even *talked* to me in weeks. Mrs. D squats down next to me and uses her quietest voice. "I like that you get so absorbed in your work, Meena," she says, "but sometimes your daydreaming gets in the way of being a good listener."

I grip the crayon in my hand. "I just didn't hear you," I say.

She makes her disappointed face.

I put my forehead down on my arms. Mrs. D stays there a few seconds longer before she stands up and walks away.

It's not fair. I didn't do anything! I sneak a look over my arms at the behavior chart. At the start of the day, all our clothespins started out in the middle, at Ready for Anything. But I clipped down to Think About Your Choices for giving myself a Magic Marker manicure during social studies. Now my clothespin is all the way down to Last Chance!

But one clip is sitting way up at the top of the chart, next to At My Best.

Sofía clipped up three times today. First, she held the door for the Milk Crate Carriers without being asked. Second, she waited to be excused for recess instead of running to the door when the bell rang. Third, she used her markers responsibly in social studies by coloring her map extra neatly instead of her fingernails.

Our clips have been going in different directions all year.

Sofía and I used to be a team. She made sure I remembered my homework, and I made sure she didn't get caught walking across the top rungs of the monkey bars. She reminded me to give other kids a turn on the swing, and I reminded her that she could use glitter crayons to fill in her pie charts. She made me practice my spelling words, and I made her laugh hard enough to snort strawberry milk through her nose.

But ever since we got back from winter break, she's been avoiding me. It's not like we used to spend every minute together before. She usually played four square at morning recess while I played kickball. She and Nora pranced their horse figurines around during afternoon recess while Pedro and I ran races.

Middle recess was *ours*, though. Every day, for three years, Sofía and I jumped rope or played freeze tag or just sat in the tube slide and talked.

Lately she stays in for Catch Up Club instead of coming out for recess with me. I don't know why. It's just for kids who have makeup work to do, and

Sofía's so smart, she could probably leave for college tomorrow. Every time she stays in to work, my stomach feels hot and bubbly, like one of those volcanoes that's just been sitting there for ages but maybe, someday, could blow.

Now even her portrait is better than mine. I bury my face back in my arms.

"I have an exciting new project for you to think about over the weekend," I hear Mrs. D say. "This one is for Valentine's Day."

About half the class cheers when she says that. The other half groans. I'm in the groany half. Most of our exciting new projects are really just homework in disguise. We probably have to write a poem about L-O-V-E or do fractions with candy hearts.

But Mrs. D's very next words make my head spring back up. "You're all going to decorate your own valentine box."

Decorating is my best subject!

Sofía whips her head around and looks at me with bright eyes, and for just a second my stomach does a swoop. I almost smile at her.

Then my brain catches up.

We don't do projects together anymore.

I scowl. The light in Sofía's eyes fizzles out. She turns back around in her desk.

"I want you to use your imagination," Mrs. D says. "Be as creative as you want. Come up with something to *wow* me. The sky's the limit."

My hand shoots in the air. "What's the prize if you win?" I say.

Mrs. D does an extra-long blink. "It's not a contest, Meena."

"Yeah, but if yours just happens to be the best, what do you get?"

"You get a box full of valentines, like everyone else. And the satisfaction of a job well done." Mrs. D checks the clock. "You can bring your boxes to school as soon as they're finished. Just make sure they're here in time for our Valentine's Day party next Friday."

I sneak another peek at Sofía's clothespin. Prize or no prize, somebody's going to make the best valentine box in the class. Sofía might have perfect handwriting. She might have eyes that stay on her paper and feet that stay under her desk. She might want to be alone at the top of the clip chart more than she wants to be my friend.

But my valentine box will be better than hers.

It's my turn to be At My Best.

2

What are you going to make?" Eli asks me when school gets out. The sun is so bright that for a second we can hardly see.

"I don't know yet," I say. I blink against the light a bunch of times until I see Sofía's mom standing at the end of the sidewalk, waiting. She's wearing her soft black shawl with roses stitched along the edges. It looks like Sofía's Rose Garden.

I used to love when she'd wrap me up in one of her big shawl hugs. We never talked much, because I hardly know any Spanish, and her English is hard to understand. But when I went over to Sofía's, her mom would always look at me with smiling eyes, hold the door wide open, and say my name like a song.

I feel a squeeze in my chest thinking about it. I don't want to walk by her now. She hangs so many of Sofía's worksheets on their refrigerator, you can't even tell what color it is. She always makes Sofía sit right down and do her homework after school, too. Maybe she's the reason Sofía decided to stay in for recess to do extra work instead of coming out to play.

I tug on Eli's sleeve and pull him in a different direction. "This way," I say.

Eli and I would probably be friends even if we weren't related. He always has muddy circles or grass stains on his jeans, which is my favorite kind of kid.

We cut across to the playground, our jackets flapping open while we run. It's been warm enough this week to melt the snow into icy stepping-stones in the grass. We start leaping from one to another.

Ever since winter break, the sky has been hazy, and the snow has been shrunken and dirty. It's the worst snow of all—too dry to build with, too crusty

to leave footprints. It's the kind that just lies there in sheets making everything gray. That's how I've been feeling since Sofía stopped being my friend. Hazy. Small. Walking out into fog every day makes me feel like I'm drowning in gray.

But today the sky is bright blue. The sun flashes off the ice and ripples all around us. When we're halfway across the playground, we stop and look around. The ground between the patches of snow is still brown, but when I take a big breath, I can smell the mud warming up all around us. Mom says it's nowhere near spring, but maybe she's wrong. Maybe the sun will keep melting the ugly snow and turn everything green and colorful again. Maybe it will clear away the gray haze that seeps into me every time I see Sofía. Maybe it will even give me the courage to ask why she isn't my friend anymore.

I tip my head and stare up at the sky so all I see is blue.

"You don't even have an *idea* how to decorate your box?" Eli asks. "That's not like you."

"Not yet," I say, breathing in deep, filling up on blue. "Do you?"

"Yep."

"Really? Already? What?"

"You'll see. I need some glue, though. The good stuff." He looks at me sideways. "Can I borrow yours?"

"You know I'm not allowed to bring that to school anymore."

"Well, that's weird, because *somebody* glued my container of crackers shut before lunch."

I giggle. "I shared my Flaming Crunchers with you."

"That's why I wasn't mad." He holds out his hand.

I shrug off my backpack and reach inside, past wadded-up papers and wrappers and socks. There are crumbs at the bottom that used to be graham crackers and sticky suckers I'm still planning to finish. Finally, I feel the zipper of my pencil bag. I pull it open and take out my secret bottle of You-Must-Be-Crazy Glue. "Just don't tell anyone," I say. "And don't get it on your fingers. And if it drips, be careful where you set it down, because it will pretty much live there forever."

Eli reaches. I hold it behind my back. "Trade you," I say.

He grins, then he digs into his pocket, pulls out a foil packet of Banana Burst gum, and pops out a little square. My mouth starts to water at the thought of the fruity explosion. We trade, and I slip it in my pocket for later. I want to chew it now, but Mom doesn't believe in sugar-full gum, and she can smell it from a mile away.

We start hopping again. The light keeps

flickering across the ice as we go. It almost looks like sparks—like the sun is setting the ice on fire.

It's pretty, but it's also making me dizzy. My head is woozy, and everything is starting to spin. Eli is getting farther and farther ahead of me. "You coming?" he calls back to me.

I need to stop and rub my eyes.

And just like that, Eli is standing in front of me again. He was ahead of me. I just saw him! Now he's right here, frowning. Blurry.

"What are you staring at?" he asks.

My head feels fuzzy. I taste metal, just like when Mrs. D flashed across the room. "Nothing," I say. I blink a few times, trying to focus.

We start hopping again, but I'm off balance for some reason. I can usually beat Eli, but I can't seem to keep up anymore. I try to concentrate. I keep my head down, my eyes on my feet, but I keep landing on the melted edges of the ice instead of the dry spots in the middle.

By the time we make it across the soccer field, my head is feeling better, but my feet are cold and wet and sloshing around inside my shoes.

This is the spot where Eli goes right and I go left. He starts walking backward away from me. "You want to come over tomorrow?" he asks.

That perks me up a little. "Can we work on our igloo?" I say. "I picked up a whole bunch more milk jugs. We might have enough to start on the roof."

"Sure," he says. "See you later." He heads off down the street.

I stamp my wet feet on the sidewalk and turn the other way. My house is only a few blocks from here, and now that I'm a third grader, I'm allowed to walk by myself, as long as I go straight home and stay on the sidewalk.

I do most of those things, most of the time—except on recycling day, when I might accidentally stop and fill my backpack with cool stuff from the bins.

Today I take my time walking. The fuzziness in my head is almost gone. I breathe the tinny smell of the melting snow, listen to icicles drip from the houses and the water trickling in the eaves. Once in a while a car drives by, and the tires make a sticky sound on the street.

I start playing my walking game: trying to spot every color of the rainbow. I made it up a few weeks ago. Every time Sofía stayed inside for recess again instead of playing with me, I felt sad and gray, like someone had pulled a plug and drained out all the colors in the world. I started *looking* for color on my way home. I imagined sucking it in through a straw. I felt it feeding me, lighting me up from the inside, coating me like invisible armor.

Today, with the bright blue sky and the

diamond sparkle of ice, I feel less starved for color, but I want to fill the rest of the way up. I see a slash of orange spray paint where the sidewalk is broken and a tuft of green in the dead grass. Two colors, right off the bat! I head to the street to look for more. There's a drink lid caught in some mucky leaves in the gutter. I watch the water swirl around it in a little stream. The water makes a metallic echo as it drizzles down through a grate.

This lid isn't the kind of trash I like. It's litter. Litter is icky and soggy. A lot of it used to be in someone's mouth—straws and flossers and cigarette butts. Sometimes those things can surprise you, though. Once I saw a Band-Aid that looked like it was holding the sidewalk together at the crack. Another time I saw a wad of gum that looked exactly like a brain.

If you pick up enough litter, sometimes you find something really great. People are always getting rid of stuff just because it's no good at doing one thing, even though it's still great for lots of other uses.

Some people even do that with their friends.

Not me. I save everything useful or beautiful. DVDs still reflect like moonbeams when they're scratched. Christmas lights still look like jewels when they're burned out. Paper clips still have lots of bend in them when they're broken in half.

I fish the lid out of the gutter and keep counting colors. It doesn't take long to find the whole rainbow. In a few minutes I have a drippy yellow grocery bag, a smashed red paper cup, a blue bottle lid, and there—a purple mitten by the curb! I stick the mitten in my backpack and carry everything else to a nearby trash bin. I lift the lid and stop.

I have to look again, because I can't even believe what I see.

A pink feather scarf is sitting on top of the trash bags inside. I look around, but nobody is coming for it. I drop all the litter to one side and try to pull out the scarf, but it's caught on something. The bin and I play tug-of-war for a while, but then I give the scarf a good yank, it comes free, and I fly backward and land on the ground.

I stare at the scarf in my hands. It's stringy and crunchy, and half the feathers are gone.

Also, it kind of smells like tuna.

But it's *beautiful*.

I drape it over my shoulders. This thing makes me feel like a movie star! I just know I'll use it to make something great, as soon as I get an Inspiration. With awesome stuff like this, I'll *definitely* make a better valentine box than Sofía!

I pick myself up and run down the sidewalk, letting the scarf trail behind me. Then I grab hold of both ends and jump rope with it all the way home.

Mom!"

She's typing at the kitchen table when I run into the house. "Shoes," Mom says without looking up.

I kick my sneakers toward the shoe rack and drop my jacket on the floor. I cram the feather scarf into my backpack too, because in my experience, Mom doesn't appreciate beautiful things that smell like tuna.

"Jacket," Mom sings as I head for the fridge.

I groan and hang it up.

"Hands," she calls out when I try for the fridge again.

"They're clean!"

Mom tips her head down and smirks at me over the top of her glasses.

Okay, so this is not my first time picking up litter.

I wash up and shovel a few grapes into my mouth, because I'm feeling a little low on purple.

It'd be a lot easier to eat the rainbow if Mom would just give in and buy gummy bears, but at least she gets lots of different colors of fruits and vegetables. I bounce on my toes next to her while she clicks for another minute, adding numbers to a chart on her screen.

Finally, she turns to me, hair springing out of her ponytail. Her hug smells like black-jelly-bean tea. "Okay, let's have it," she says with a smile. "Tell me everything."

"Did you see the snow is melting?" I say.

"I sure did."

"And something dripped in the driveway that's making a rainbow splotch where we park the car, and I bet tomorrow we'll have enough milk jugs to finish our igloo, and Mrs. D said we can make our own valentine boxes!"

"Oooh, you do like a project." Mom leans closer. "You want some ideas?"

I make a snorting sound. "From you?"

"What? I'm good at projects."

"You're the *worst* at projects."

"But I draw up a mean balance sheet. Would that help?"

"Mom."

"Fine, then. I'll just be on your snack committee." She leans back in her chair. "Do you want to have anybody over to work on it with you?"

I know this is her way of asking why Sofía hasn't been over lately. But how do you tell your own mom that your best friend doesn't hang out with you anymore? I scratch the back of my neck. "I think we're supposed to work alone," I say.

Mom raises an eyebrow at me. "Since when do you pay attention to the rules?"

I shrug.

She sighs. "Suit yourself."

"Hey," I ask, trying to change the subject, "do you think there are any other dads in my class with size fourteen feet?"

"I doubt that very much."

"That means I'll have the biggest box in the class!" I pop the last grape into my mouth, grab my backpack, and run for the stairs.

I stop short when I get to the living room. My little sister only has kindergarten in the morning, so she's been home with Mom all afternoon. She's watching her show about the alphabet or cooperation or whatever. I'll have to sneak past her if I want a chance to work by myself. I drop down on my hands and knees and crawl behind the couch, all the way to the stairs. I sneak halfway up, super quiet, then race the rest of the way to my workshop.

I'm the only kid I know who has my own workshop. It was supposed to be Rosie's room, but she didn't like sleeping alone, so a few weeks ago they moved her bed back into my room, and we made this my project space instead. That way the mess stays all in one place.

Everything in my workshop is just the way I like it. The floor is covered in paper scraps. Flattened cereal boxes that say things like "Now with more fiber!" are piled in the corner. Beautiful trash is spilling out of crates: bottle caps, keys that don't open anything, a syrup bottle shaped like a lady, Popsicle sticks stained orange or cherry or grape.

They're all just waiting to be used.

I drop my backpack, peel off my wet socks, and kick some stuff out of the way to make space on the floor, because it's hard to work around all those bottles of You-Must-Be-Crazy Glue stuck to my table. I dump the candy wrappers I've been saving out of my biggest shoe box, all over the floor.

Time to get to work.

I pull the feather scarf out of my backpack and wind it around my neck. I flip on my walkie-talkie in case it picks up trucker voices. I pop the Banana Burst gum into my mouth and imagine the gooey explosion of fruit flavor filling me with sunshine yellow.

Now I'm ready. I lie on my back, hold the empty

box up over my head, and stare into it, waiting for Inspiration.

I wish I'd gotten to show Sofía this place. I made it just like the Craft Center from when we were in kindergarten. There were lots of great things to do back then. You could build with blocks or bang on drums or shovel dry corn in a bin, but I almost always picked the Craft Center. I loved pounding clay and squirting glue and tearing up bits of paper then taping them back together. Sometimes I'd spend my whole snack time daydreaming about what I might make later.

That's where I met Sofía. She'd hardly said a word during class, and from the way Pedro talked to her, I wasn't sure she knew English. Then one morning she came to the Craft Center and sat bent over her paper, drawing pictures in pencil.

Pencil! All those crayons and markers and chalk, and she picked a plain old pencil!

I was squeezing globs of paint onto a huge sheet of paper from the roll. When Sofía looked up at me, I smeared my hands through the paint and gave her a big wave—orange with one hand and yellow with the other. Then I pushed the paper over to her. I didn't know how to say "You want a turn?" in Spanish, so I raised my eyebrows and pointed.

Sofía looked at the paper, then at me. I nodded.

She touched the paint with the tip of her finger and traced a little line. I wiped a big streak across the page to show her how. Finally, Sofía gave me a shy smile and pressed her whole hand into the glob of paint. I smacked mine down next to hers and splattered us both with orange. The next thing you know, we were smearing and giggling and splattering.

It turns out you don't have to use any words at all to make something beautiful together.

We spent every day at the Craft Center after that. She knew plenty of English, once you got her talking. We drew pictures of each other. We raced to see who could color a page the fastest. We cut paper into confetti and threw it in the air. We even learned how to vacuum! And outside at recess, we ran races together and climbed the monkey bars and hurled playground balls at each other.

But it seems like every year one of my favorite parts of school disappears. In first grade they took away the Craft Center and gave us spelling tests. In second grade they took away show-and-tell and gave us multiplication. This year they took away snack time and gave us cursive. Sofía doesn't mind. She's the world's leading expert on third grade.

I was better at kindergarten.

My workshop is the one place I can still do

everything I love. It doesn't matter if your clip is always going the wrong way and your letters don't look like the handwriting chart and you keep forgetting to use your inside voice.

And even though it was *supposed* to be more like a clubhouse, even though Sofía and I were *supposed* to use it together, I am not letting this place go to waste.

"Meena?"

I hear the door to my workshop creaking open.

That didn't take long. "You're supposed to knock," I say.

Rosie pulls the door closed again and gives a little tap.

I grin. "Who is it?"

"It's Rosie," she says.

"You can come in, but I'm working."

Rosie pushes the door open. She's carrying her pink plastic pony by the tail, and the hair Dad put up in a little blond sprout this morning is off to the side. She must have had a nap after school.

I turn back to stare into my box some more.

"What's in there?" she asks.

"Nothing yet."

Rosie lies down on her back next to me and looks up into the box. After a while she sits up and starts fiddling with the candy wrappers on the floor all around us. She scoops them up and lets them fall. Some of them are clear red from cinnamon candies. Others are shiny gold from butter toffees. There are even silver ones that still smell like chocolate. How could anybody ever throw those away?

"Watch this," I say. I set down the shoe box, lie on my back, and swish my arms and legs over the floor. The wrappers make a crinkly sound all around me. I stand up again. "See," I say. "It's an angel."

Rosie's face lights up. "Me too!"

I mess up the wrappers again. Rosie plops down in the middle and swishes. I grab her hand and help her up. She giggles at the Rosie-size angel on the floor.

That's when I get my Inspiration.

I sit back down, grab my last not-stuck bottle of You-Must-Be-Crazy Glue, and stick a gold wrapper to the outside of my box. I stick on a silver one. Then a red one. Rosie sits and watches while I start covering the whole box with wrappers.

"What are you making?" she asks.

"I don't know," I say. Because I don't. Not yet. All I know is that I'm going to need all the candy wrappers I can get.

It turns out this is why I was saving them.

I think about my valentine box as soon as I wake up on Saturday. Before I even open my eyes, I remember how pretty it looked all covered with candy wrappers.

I can't wait to see what I'll do next!

I get up and pull on my tie-dyed hoodie. It's stretchy and comfy and covers me in a rainbow right away so the gray haze can't even *think* about seeping in. My hoodie's also great for making art, because no one can tell if I smear markers or paint on it. I creep across the room. Rosie makes a snuffling sound, so I wait until she starts sleep-breathing again and then slip out the door.

Pale yellow light is shining through the window in my workshop. There's a circle of fog in the middle of the glass. I call that my Magic Mist. It only appears on cold mornings, and only until the house gets warm, so it's a perfect spot to make secret little wishes or ask questions, like you do with those Magic 8-Balls. This one time I thought

I might have a crush on Pedro, so I wrote "I ♥ Pedro" on the Magic Mist, and just seeing it there freaked me out so much that I had to smear it away before anybody saw it and thought I actually *meant* it. It turned out I was just excited about Pedro's new backpack that had a million pockets and even a real compass attached to the zipper. So that was a close one.

But see? The Magic Mist worked just like a crystal ball!

Today I draw a big sun in the Magic Mist. I make a wish that the snow keeps melting and all the colors come flooding back and they drown out all the gray that's everywhere, inside and out, even if it *is* too early for spring. I smear out the inside of the sun to make a clear spot where there isn't any mist at all.

Now I'm ready to work on my box. I plop down on my knees and start rifling through my supplies, looking for Inspiration. I peek into every container and reach all the way down to the bottom of my bins.

That's when I feel something cold and smooth. I jerk my hand away.

I'd forgotten about this jar. But that's why I stuck it way down in the bottom of the bin, isn't it? So I'd forget?

I move aside the fluffy ends I cut off some pom-poms, reach back into the bin, and pull out the jar. I turn it over in my hands and watch the little metal bits inside clinking against the glass. Just the sight of all the aluminum can tabs makes my heart crack a little. Sofía used to pull them off her juice cans every day at lunch for me. She was the only person I ever knew who brought juice in little cans instead of boxes, and I loved how every one of those tiny metal rings was like a souvenir of our day. Even though they were just ordinary can tabs. Even though they were just ordinary days.

There are hundreds of them.

For the first few days after winter break, we still ate lunch together. She'd been gone a couple of extra days visiting family, so when she stayed in for recess, I just figured she needed to catch up on work. Sofía is one of those kids who worry how they did on a test right before they get the highest score in the class, so I knew she wouldn't relax until she had a chance to practice spelling flash cards or brush up on science vocabulary or whatever.

But she stayed inside the next day, too, and the one after that. Every recess, I missed her more. The following day, when she started to duck into the classroom on the way to recess *again*, I stopped her. "What are you even doing in there?" I asked, pinching the can tab she'd given me from her lunch. "You must be caught up by now."

Sofía looked away. "I just have some things to do."

"Well, can you come out tomorrow?"

She shrugged.

"Next *week*?"

She didn't answer.

"Hang on," I said slowly, stepping in front of the doorway. "How much longer are you planning to stay in?"

"I don't know." Sofía shifted between her feet. "It might be a while."

My mouth dropped open. "You'd rather stay inside than play with me?"

"I didn't say that."

"But I never see you anymore! Come on." I tugged on her sleeve, my heart starting to beat faster. "Let's go outside."

She pulled away.

I dropped my hand, stunned. "Don't you even want to?" I said.

"Why don't you come with me?" she said, brightening. "Mrs. D will let anyone stay in. You could work on your handwriting."

My jaw got tight. "What's wrong with my handwriting?"

Sofía bit her lip. "You could use a little more practice, right?"

Hot lava started to bubble in my stomach.

"Maybe I like my letters the way they are," I said. "Just because I don't write perfect cursive like you doesn't mean I need to miss recess."

"I'm just saying—"

"No," I huffed. "I'm not going in there. But if you have better things to do than play with me, see if I care."

She sucked in a breath and took a step back.

I crossed my arms. "Well, go ahead."

Sofía's face hardened. Her lips pressed together into a thin line. She bumped against my shoulder as she stormed into the room.

I stood there, feeling the sting all the way down to my fingers, still pinching the can tab. I turned, hurled it into the wastebasket, and stalked off down the hall.

Now, sitting on the floor of my workshop, staring at the jar of tabs, the hot-lava feeling has dulled to a warm ache. I guess Sofía plans to stay in for recess until she's the best at everything. I guess she doesn't have time anymore for people who clip down and write crooked letters and scribble on their papers without meaning to.

Well, maybe they don't have time for her, either. I shove the jar back into the bin.

I'm just sitting back on my heels when a wave of nausea swooshes through my stomach.

I gasp. An even bigger wave crashes over me.

Huh. This is different from the lava. It's different from the sad feeling in my chest, too. Maybe I'm hungry. I guess I'll have some cereal before I start working on my box.

I tiptoe down the stairs. I'm the only one up, so I pour an extra-big bowl of Rainbow Pops, and nobody even asks if I checked the serving size! I fill it all the way to the rim. But right when I'm pouring the milk, my arm jerks, and I make a big sploosh on the table. I set down the jug and give my arms a shake. They've been herky and jerky in the mornings lately. Last week I karate-chopped Rosie's orange juice right off the table somehow. And yesterday I flung the toothpaste right off my brush, and I didn't even mean to!

I throw a towel over the milk spot and start scooping out all the red Pops. They don't make my stomach feel any better, so I move on to the orange ones. I've only made it to yellow when Dad comes down in his running clothes. "What's the story, morning glory?" he asks. He's wearing the sneakers that came out of my valentine box, and his pants are super tight. They make his feet look even bigger, which is saying something.

He puts a slice of bread in the toaster. "That's a pretty big bowl you've got there," he says.

"Those are pretty big feet you've got there," I mumble around my Pops.

He peeks into my bowl. "Still three colors to go, I see."

I do a big swallow. "Still bigfoot, I see." He points his toe and poses just like a shoe model, which makes me giggle. "You look like a scuba diver in that outfit," I say.

"It's not an outfit. It's *gear*."

"Then what's with the neon stripes?"

"They're so cars can see me at night."

"You don't run at night."

"Duh. It's dark then." He grabs a banana from the fruit bowl and starts to peel it. "You gonna show me your project today?"

And that's when Rainbow Pops go flying right at his face.

"Hey!" Dad says.

I gasp. I look down at my empty spoon.

"What'd you do that for?"

He grabs the towel from me and jerks it across his face.

"It was an accident," I say.

"You *accidentally* threw cereal at me?"

"I didn't mean to! My arms are still waking up."

He puts his hands on his hips.

I slump in my chair. "Fine, then I'm just clumsy, okay?"

He tosses the towel onto the table. "Nobody's that clumsy," he grumbles.

I push my bowl away. "Nobody but me."

Dad squints at me. His eyes get a little softer. "What's up with you today?" He doesn't sound mad anymore.

But I don't know how to answer. My arms do things I don't tell them to. The cereal makes my stomach feel worse, almost like—

That's when it hits me. I must be getting sick. But that's not fair! I can't get sick on a *Saturday*! Why couldn't I have gotten sick yesterday, when we had our spelling test and they served fish burgers for lunch?

I rub my eyes. My head is starting to spin, and my skin feels scratchy. I peel off my hoodie and drop it on the floor. Maybe I just need to lie down. I slide out of my chair, but the couch seems so far away, and I'm too dizzy to make it. I sink down onto the kitchen floor.

"Hey," Dad says, coming around the table. "Are you okay?" He crouches next to me.

I'm not okay. Not at all. My stomach is worse than ever, and now the room is going around and around. I curl up into a ball.

"Let's get you back to bed," Dad says.

He starts to scoop me up, but I moan and pull away. I don't want anything to touch me. My skin is stinging, and my stomach gives the biggest lurch of all.

"Meena?"

His voice sounds far away and hollow, like he's talking through a pipe. I can smell his toast burning. I squeeze my eyes shut until all I see is the darkness behind my lids. . . .

Meena?"

I open my eyes. Mom is leaning over me, her body outlined in a ring of bright light. The burnt-toast smell is gone. Now it smells like those Band-Aids with the medicine already inside.

Where am I?

I'm in a bed with rails. I start to sit up, but the room sways like a teeter-totter. I lie back down and feel something catch on my finger.

I gasp and jerk away. "It's okay," Mom says, rubbing my arm. "She's just taking your pulse." Mom guides my hand over to a lady who fastens a clip to the tip of my finger. It looks like the clothes-pins we use at school, except there's a teeny light at the end and a cord coming out the side.

A machine next to the bed starts beeping, and I jump. "That's just your heartbeat," Mom says, squeezing my hand. The number "91" lights up on a display. I slump against the pillow. Mom starts to stroke my hair, but it makes my head hurt. I moan and turn away.

Dad is here too, on the other side of the bed. "What's the story, morning glory?" he says, leaning in close to me. Didn't he already say that? He's wearing his running clothes, which is weird, because he's not allowed to wear those outside the house unless he is actually running. Which reminds me . . .

He was getting ready to go for a run.

I was getting ready to work on my box.

How did we end up here?

There's no color at all in this place. Everything is white and beige. My eyes dart around the room. There's a hard floor and a sink and some cabinets and a curtain hanging from the ceiling that looks like it could whoosh around with just a little tug and close me up in a white cocoon. My heart starts to rattle around in my chest.

But just then Dad holds up something in front of my face that fills me with color. "Do you remember this guy?" he says.

I squint until the colors take shape in Dad's hand. It's a stuffed zebra with rainbow stripes. I've never seen him before, but right away I know his name should be Raymond. "Where did he come from?" I ask. My voice sounds scratchy, like I haven't been using it.

"They gave him to you in the ambulance," Dad says.

My stomach tightens like a wad of crumpled paper. "What ambulance?"

"The one that drove you here."

Is this a hospital? Is that where I am? I don't realize my heart is beating faster until the beeps coming from the machine speed up. "What happened?" I ask.

"You had a seizure, honey," Mom says.

A seizure. I don't know that word. It sounds like "sea" and "treasure" mixed together: SEA-sure. But my head is still full of static, and my stomach is shriveling up, and it's hard to think. "What's that?" I ask.

"It's something that happens in your brain," the lady next to Mom says.

My breath gets caught in my throat. "My brain?"

The lady rolls a little stool over to the bed and sits so her face is just over the top of the rails. She has on one of those shirts that nurses wear. It's blue with alligators swimming in all different directions. "You know what your brain does, don't you?" she asks.

My heart is beating in my ears, and the machine is beeping fast. I'm so scared, I can't even think about what my brain does. My teeth start to chatter. I clamp them together and take a big breath. I remember now. "It's in charge of your body," I say to her.

She nods. "That's right." Her eyes are brown and marbled, like tree bark. "Your brain is kind of like the president of the body. It gives all the orders and makes sure everything else is doing its job."

I nod. Her explanation makes me think of my portrait of President Meena. I imagine her sitting at a big desk inside my head. She has rainbow hair and not even one purple scribble on her face, and she's calling into a megaphone: *Heart! Keep up that beating. Lungs! Don't forget to breathe. Everybody come on up here later for cake.*

"That's what your brain is supposed to do," the nurse is saying. "But during a seizure, your brain goes off track. It stops sending messages that make sense and just sends random impulses instead. It sort of sparks. Like fireworks."

I blink at her a few times. "You mean my head lit up?"

"No, sweetheart," Mom says. "But you couldn't talk, and you couldn't hear us, and your body started shaking."

"I was shaking?" I ask.

"Not for very long," Dad says.

I start twisting up the edge of the sheet. "Then why don't I remember it?"

"Most people don't," the nurse says.

"Were you guys shaking too?"

Mom and Dad look at each other. "No, honey," Mom says.

"What about Rosie?" I look around, then sit up with a jolt. "What happened to Rosie? Where is she?" The beeps speed up again.

"She's fine," Mom says, easing me back down. "I took her to Eli's."

Just then something starts squeezing my arm. I whip my head around and see a band on my arm getting tighter and tighter.

Dad lays a hand on my head. "That's just taking your blood pressure."

But it's clamping down hard. "It's crushing me," I say, wriggling against it. I swat and claw at it with my other hand, and I'm just about to yell "stop" when it loosens up. For a long minute I hold my breath while the machine next to the bed hums and ticks. Finally, the band makes a sighing sound and lets go.

"One twenty over sixty," the nurse says. "That's actually not bad, considering."

I slump back onto the bed. My head is pounding too much to wonder what those numbers mean. It feels like President Meena is inside my skull, hammering to get out. It reminds me of those fireworks that boom so loud, you have to cover your ears—the ones that create a puff of smoke instead of something beautiful.

I hate that kind.

"So, she hasn't had a fever?" I hear the nurse say.

"She's been fine," Mom replies.

"Any blows to the head? Did you get hit by a kickball yesterday, Meena? Maybe knock your head on the monkey bars?"

I shake my head no.

"Do you remember what you did at recess?"

I can hardly think through the pounding. But then I get a flash, remembering the back of Eli's jacket. I was reaching for it. We were running. "I played tag," I say.

"Any toxins she might have been exposed to?" the nurse asks Mom and Dad. "Lead paint? Pest-control products?"

"No, nothing," Mom says.

"Fish burgers," I mumble. Everyone turns to look at me. "We had fish burgers for lunch."

Dad gives me a little punch in the arm. "You packed your own lunch yesterday."

"Yeah, but I bet just the smell is toxic."

The nurse grins while she clicks on a computer. "How about video games? Do you play anything with a lot of flashing lights?"

Mom is shaking her head. "All she did yesterday was work on an art project."

That's when I remember something. "The ice," I say.

The nurse looks up.

"When I was walking home with my cousin Eli," I tell her. "The sun was shining on the ice. It was all bright and dazzling. It made me so dizzy, I had to look away." The nurse nods slowly at me. She types something into the computer. "Does that mean anything?" I ask.

"We'll see." She closes her computer and stands. "We're just putting down everything we can think of right now, okay? I'm glad you told us about the ice."

Just then I feel a big wave of I'm-gonna-be-sick. I roll onto my side and hug my stomach. "I don't feel good," I say, sucking in as much air as I can.

"We can give you something for that," the nurse says, "but we need to check a few things first. Do you think you can hold on a little bit longer?"

I squeeze my eyes shut and nod.

"Good. We'll get you through just as quick as we can. The doctor ordered a CT scan," she says, turning to Mom again, "and we'll need to draw some blood to check her insulin levels." The nurse unhooks the clip from my finger. The machine next to me stops beeping. "Right now we're going for a little ride, Meena." She gets behind the bed and starts pushing.

I grab hold of the rails. I didn't know this thing was on wheels! "Hang on," I say, reaching for Mom. "You're coming with me, aren't you?"

Mom gives the nurse a worried look.

"She'll be right outside," the nurse says to me. "The scan won't take long. Can you be a trooper for us?"

I swallow.

Mom gives my hand a hard squeeze. Then she pulls it up to her lips, kisses it, and lets me go. She brushes the hair off my forehead. "You can do it, kiddo," she says, blinking fast. "You've got this." She smoothes down the front of my pajama shirt.

The nurse starts wheeling the bed toward the white hallway. The front of my shirt goes cold.

"Wait!" I say. "Where's my hoodie?" I look all over the room, but I don't see it anywhere. I start gasping for air.

"I think it's at home," Dad says.

"Can you get it? I need it!"

"Meena, we're twenty minutes away. You'll be done before you know it."

I can't go rolling off into all that white without *something*! "What about Raymond?" I say, thinking fast. "Can he come?"

Nobody says anything at first. They all just look at me. Then finally Dad leans in closer. "Sorry, who?"

I grab the rainbow-striped zebra out of his hands and clutch him against my chest. "Raymond." I turn to the nurse. "I'm bringing him."

She smiles. "You got it."

I press Raymond right up to my face. I take a deep, shaky breath that goes all the way through to his stuffing. I suck in all the color I can from his rainbow stripes. Then I lie back down as the nurse starts pushing the bed toward the door.

I hold tight to Raymond and watch the ceiling tiles pass by while she wheels us out of the room.

6

We get home from the hospital in time for lunch. There are muddy footprints on the kitchen floor. There are dirty tracks where it looks like something was wheeled through. There's a bowl of gray mush on the table that used to be Rainbow Pops. Mom starts cleaning up right away, like she wants to erase what happened.

That would be fine by me.

My hoodie is thrown over a chair. I set Raymond down long enough to pull the sweatshirt on, then I tuck him under my arm while I get a pair of scissors. I wedge the point under the plastic bracelet they put on me at the hospital. I really have to work the scissors, making one little notch at a time until finally I cut the whole thing clean off.

It was much easier cutting off the bracelet Sofía made me. I thought that thing would last forever. But it turns out rubber bands disintegrate after a while, even if you remember not to chew on them when you practice your handwriting. Maybe that's what happened to the one I made her. Maybe that's why she stopped wearing it after our fight.

Or maybe not.

"We should get you some lunch," Dad says, coming up behind me and easing the scissors out of my hand. "What do you want?"

I slump into the chair and put my head on the table. "Nothing." My stomach is finally better, but even with my hoodie on, I feel drab and wilted, like all the colors have been wrung right out of me. I squeeze Raymond.

"How about mac and cheese?" Dad asks.

I shrug.

"How about *green* mac and cheese?"

My head shoots back up. Mac and cheese is okay. But add a few drops of blue food coloring, and *whamo*—it looks like a pot of slugs! "You'd really make that for me?" I ask.

"Sure, why not? You're supposed to eat the rainbow, right?"

"You're *supposed* to eat spinach," Mom says, dumping the gray mush into the sink. "And tomatoes and squash—"

"—and jelly beans and sprinkles and green mac and cheese!" I say.

She sighs and gives me a tired smile. "In moderation."

"We should all have some!"

"Not on your life," she says. "Why don't you go lie down for a bit?"

I groan.

"Maybe you could watch something until lunch is ready."

I stare at her. Green mac and cheese *and* screen time? They didn't even make me do my homework first! I wonder if I could get anything else out of this little situation here. "Any chance we could have cream soda with lunch?" I ask.

Mom raises an eyebrow at me. I bat my eyelashes at her until she smirks. "Just this once," she says.

I hop up and start to run for the living room. Only just in time, I think maybe I should take it a little slower, in case they're watching. As soon as I'm out of sight, I bounce onto the couch.

I don't know what to watch first! There's this show where monster trucks drive over and flatten cars, or videos of a guy who pumps electricity through his body until his hair starts to smoke. There's even an eat-or-be-eaten series where Eli always roots for the gazelles and I cheer for the lions. I've just made up my mind and settled under the blanket with Raymond when Rosie runs in, dragging Pink Pony by the mane.

"Meena!" she yells. She's still wearing her

nightgown, and her hair is springing out every which way.

"Hey, squirt," I say.

Rosie runs over and slams me with a hug. I hug her back, but she doesn't let go. She just hangs from my neck for so long that I have to tap her on the shoulder. "It's getting kinda hard to breathe here," I say.

She finally sets me free. But then she drops Pink Pony, puts her hands on my cheeks, and looks at me with big eyes. "You rode in an ambulance," she says.

She's so serious, but I can't help it, I smile. The way she says "am-blee-ance" is kind of cute. "I know," I say.

"Was it scary?"

"Nah." She looks so impressed that I forget to mention that I don't remember the ride.

"It was for me," she says.

Rosie climbs onto the couch and slides under the blanket to sit right next to me. She leans her head on my shoulder, holds on to Pink Pony by the tail, and starts sucking her fingers.

Until this moment I hadn't thought about what Rosie saw. It's weird that she remembers something I don't. I mean, it happened to *me*. Only, I guess it happened to her, too. Were there sirens? Did they wake her up? Did she come downstairs and see me on the kitchen floor, shaking and not responding to anything? Did she watch whoever made those muddy footprints when they came and took me away? I want to ask her, but by the way she's sucking on her fingers like she does after she's has a bad dream, I'm not sure I want to know.

I wonder how I'd feel if an ambulance drove away with her.

I was going to watch my monster truck show. I was all set for those big, noisy trucks stampeding over one another in the mud.

But now it feels like something is nibbling at my stomach, and I don't want to watch anything big or exciting or loud.

So I put on Rosie's favorite show instead. I cuddle against her with Raymond, pull the blanket up to my chin, and stare at the screen while cartoon dragons count pieces of pie.

My stomach still has that gnawing feeling when Dad calls us for lunch. But when I see how slimy the green slugs look today, it starts to growl a little. There's fruit salad with all the other colors in it too. I dig right in and load my plate with strawberries and pineapple and orange slices and grapes. The fruit explodes into juicy deliciousness in my mouth, and I wash it down with a cup of cream soda that fizzes in my face when I swallow.

There's nothing like a colorful lunch to make you feel twinkly and cheerful again. That's just how I need to feel to work on my valentine box! I shovel in the last bite of macaroni and push back my chair.

"Where are you going?" Mom asks.

"To my workshop."

She starts to stand up. "You want me to come?"

I stare at her. "No. . . ."

She and Dad glance sideways at each other. "Why don't you work here?" Dad says. "We can help you bring some things down."

I look around the kitchen. The counters are clear. The footprints are mopped up. There's not even anything on the refrigerator—no drawings or worksheets or report cards. This is the room where Mom usually works, and she says she can't think straight unless everything is picked up and put away.

But I don't want to think straight. I want to think swirly—in colors and patterns and textures. All this clean, empty space makes me feel blank inside. "I want to work upstairs," I say.

"I know, hon," Mom says with a sigh. "I just think we should keep an eye on you for a while."

"But I feel fine," I say. I do. Now that I'm back home and full of the rainbow, everything feels the same as always. But they're both just sitting there looking at me, frowning, like they think fireworks might start going off in my head again. The sparkly excitement starts to drain out through my fingertips. "Okay," I say in a small voice.

We all go upstairs and come back down with our arms full of supplies, spreading them out on the kitchen table. I set Raymond down next to me so he can watch. My box still has a few bare spots, so I start gluing candy wrappers over them. Mom taps away at her computer, but she keeps peeking at me over the screen. Dad loads plates into the dishwasher, but he keeps coming over to ruffle my hair.

All the looking and touching makes the nipping feeling start up in my stomach again. Not only that, but somebody brought down my jar of Sofía's can tabs, and they're just sitting there on the table, staring at me like everyone else. I try making a tunnel around my face with my hands so all I can see is my box. I stare at it, waiting for Inspiration.

Yesterday I thought the wrappers were starting to look like scales. But they just look wrinkled and messy to me now. They make my box look like trash.

Mom takes off her glasses, closes her computer, and turns to Dad. "Sleep deprivation," she says. "It's the only trigger that makes any sense. What time did she get up this morning?"

Dad flings a dish towel over his shoulder. "Not much earlier than me."

"Well, nothing else fits. There's alcohol. Head trauma. Fever. Diabetes, but they checked for that."

Dad leans against the counter. "Maybe it was just a one-time thing."

"Maybe," Mom says. She rubs her eyes.

"What about exercise? Do we have to restrict her activity?" he asks her.

"It doesn't sound like it. Exercise might even help."

Dad nods and hooks his hand on the back of his neck. When he sees me watching him, he lets go of his neck, gives me a quick smile, and takes a step toward me.

I grab Raymond and hop down from the table before anybody can ruffle my hair again. "I'm going to Eli's," I say, heading for the door.

"Hang on," Mom says. She pushes her chair back from the table. "I'll go too."

"I can get there by myself," I say, gritting my teeth.

"I know you can, but—" She looks sideways at Dad and gets up. "But I haven't had a chance to talk to Aunt Kathy all week."

It's cool and foggy out when we head to Eli's. Our shoes crunch over gritty bits of sand and salt on the sidewalk. I keep Raymond tucked under my arm while the trash bag I'm carrying thumps against my back.

Mom walks next to me in a straight line. She doesn't veer off to look in the gutter. She doesn't even slow down when we pass a red bottle cap or an orange twist tie, even though my fingers are just *itching* to pick them up.

Of course Rosie just *had* to come along, even though she spent all morning there. She keeps doing that thing where she runs ahead, stops to look at something on the sidewalk and falls behind, then runs ahead again. Usually it's kind of cute, but today, every time she runs past me, I grit my teeth so hard that they hurt.

I tighten my grip on the trash bag. Water trickles into the drain, and the sound makes me feel like we're walking into yesterday. It almost feels like I could walk right back to the spot before any of this happened, and maybe this time it wouldn't.

My aunt Kathy opens the door before we even make it to the front stoop. Rosie runs right past her into the house. Aunt Kathy is wearing the fuzzy purple sweater I love, and she opens her arms and pulls me into a big plushy hug that smells like angel food. Even though it feels good to be wrapped up in that purple softness, it starts getting a little too tight in there. Aunt Kathy gives me one last crush before I pry myself away. "Where's Eli?" I ask.

"Waiting for you," she says.

"Is it safe?"

"As safe as it gets. I think he made Rosie help him clean up this morning."

That makes me smile a little. Eli's room gets pretty stinky sometimes. But when I get to his doorway, all I smell is wood shavings and kibble. Rosie is already sticking her fingers through a cage, trying to pet Eli's rabbit. "Anybody wake up dead today?" I ask, dropping my trash bag by the door.

Eli looks up and grins. "No, but Rosie just about pet the fur off Vernon," he says, nodding toward the rabbit, who's keeping too far back for Rosie to reach. Eli goes back to dribbling something into a glass tank. "What the heck happened to you?"

I bounce the toe of my sneaker on the floor and

shrug. "What you heard." I know Aunt Kathy must have told him, but I don't want to talk about waking up in the hospital or about the test or about all the looking and touching since then. Eli and I might play tag and hunt for trash and build things together, but we don't talk about stuff like that. I hold out Raymond instead and say, "They gave me this."

Eli looks at Raymond. He nods. "Cool," he says, and goes back to feeding his gerbil. I know he'd never blab to anyone about Raymond because he still keeps a scrap of his baby blanket under his pillow. He won't tell anyone about this morning, either. The nice thing about Eli is that if I don't mention going to the hospital, he'll pretend it never happened, just like I pretend he doesn't get tears in his eyes during that show when the lion catches the gazelle.

I let out a breath and look around. It's like Eli's own personal nature center in here. There are cages and tanks and aquariums all over, some with glowing lights or bubbling water. Eli is allergic to cats, and Aunt Kathy isn't ready for another dog yet since their cocker spaniel died last year, but for some reason she's okay with pretty much every other kind of pet. He's got a turtle and a lizard and a hermit crab. He's got mice and hamsters and something called a chinchilla. He's even got an ant farm.

I mean, an ant farm? The boy can't have a

puppy, but Aunt Kathy lets him keep a box of *bugs* on his dresser? What's up with that?

"You want to feed Henry?" Eli asks.

"I do!" Rosie pipes up.

"She can do it," I say. "Henry peed on me last time."

"He won't if you don't pick him up."

"I don't care. I'm holding a grudge."

"Fine, then feed Lizzy."

Rosie sprinkles little cut-up carrots through the top of the hamster cage while I shake a can of fish pellets into the big aquarium. Lizzy swims out from behind her hiding place and scoops them into her mouth. (Or his. I don't know how you're supposed to tell.) When she's not eating, she spends all her time lurking in the fake weeds, ready to ambush. She's blue and feathery and glistens, but don't let that fool you, because Eli says if he put another fish in with her, she'd kill it.

When we're done, I grab the trash bag and we head for the kitchen. Eli stops at the fridge, grabs the milk, and chugs the last of it. He hands Rosie the empty jug and slides open the back door for her. I'm just about to follow them out when Mom stops me. "Where do you think you're going?"

I stop with my hand on the door and turn to where Aunt Kathy is pouring her some tea. "Outside," I say.

Mom frowns. "Were you planning to tell me?"

"Why would I tell you?"

"So I know where you are."

I blink at her. "I'm at Eli's. Which you already know, because you *followed* me here."

"But you're going outside now."

"So?"

She rubs her forehead. "I'd like to be able to see you."

I scowl at her, then back out the door and slide it closed. Mom shifts her chair right in front of it and crosses her arms.

"What's she doing?" Eli asks.

I feel my face get hot. "She's just mad because I glued her keys together," I say, which is not really a lie, because I did do that once.

Okay, twice.

I turn my trash bag upside down on the back porch and dump out all the milk jugs I've been collecting. Our igloo is more than half finished. We started it over Christmas, while Sofía was still visiting family. I was hoping she'd have a chance to work on it with us when she got back.

But she's never even seen it.

The igloo is in pretty good shape, considering it's taken us almost six weeks to get this far. There's just enough shelter on the porch that the wind can't knock it over, and real snow won't make it collapse.

We built it by stacking rows of milk jugs in a circle. The lids point in toward the middle, and the white, flat bottoms show on the outside. Since milk jugs are skinny at the top, when you stack them on their sides, the walls start to curve in the higher they get. If we pack them tight enough, they'll curve together to make a roof!

At least I hope they will.

"Do you want to stack or tape?" I ask, setting Raymond inside the igloo.

Eli pulls on the roll of duct tape and releases a stretchy, plastic sound. "Tape," he says. He tears off a piece, folds it over so it's sticky on both sides, slaps it onto a jug, and hands it to me.

I stack the first milk jug, making sure it sticks

to the one next to it. I have to let Rosie do the next couple, but after that she gets distracted and starts kicking a jug around in the grass. Even if she dents that one up, we should have enough to finish the igloo in a week or two, depending on how much milk the neighbors drink.

When we've stacked and taped all the jugs we have, the igloo comes up as high as my chin. We crawl through the gap we left for the door and plop down on the cold wood boards of the porch. This is my favorite part, because from the inside you can see all the different-colored lids pointing at you— blue for skim, green for low fat, red for whole. The air is chilly, but it's already warming up from our breath, and before I can stop myself, I think how much Sofía would like it in here.

At least she would have before. She always liked being tucked into small spaces. We used to hang out in the big orange tube slide at school to catch our breath after playing tag. When I went to her house, we used to pretend her hall closet was our apartment. We'd sit on the floor with the door closed drinking strawberry milk and eating sweet buns with pretty crisscross tops. If Sofía were here, she would have brought the empty jugs from her milk. We would have had pink lids too.

I hug Raymond close to me and look around the igloo at all the colors. We don't have any pink at all. One whole color is missing—one of my favorites. My stomach aches a little at the thought.

But if Sofía doesn't want to play anymore, maybe she'd just think this place was stupid.

"What do you want to do?" Eli says. "We could pretend we've just set up base camp, and we're getting ready to climb Mount Everest."

I glance out at his yard. It's brown and mucky, and there are only a couple of wimpy patches of snow left. Rosie is twirling a stick around to make a hole in one of them. "It doesn't look like a mountain," I say.

"Fine, then let's pretend we've been camping," he says, "and wolves chased us into the woods, and we're lost."

I look toward the little knot of trees at the edge of the yard. It's not exactly a forest—just a few pine trees and some scraggly bushes that nobody ever mows under. I crawl out the opening of the igloo and peek through the sliding-glass door. Mom is looking back at me, her hands wrapped around a mug. She takes a sip and gives me a little wave that makes my skin prickle.

I grit my teeth. I'd *like* to get lost. I'd go where nobody could find me and get rid of that prickly, spied-on feeling.

And just then Aunt Kathy sets a little pitcher on the table. Mom turns away from the window, picks it up, and pours something into her mug.

I don't even think before I head for the trees. The ground squishes under my feet as I hear Eli tramping behind me. I feel the watery air in my lungs. Rosie squeals a little and runs after us with Pink Pony, sensing something exciting. When we make it to the pines, I lean against a trunk, clutching Raymond to my chest and panting. I can see Eli's swing set and clotheslines through the bushes, but I can't see his back door from here. Which means Mom can't see me.

"We'll never find our way back," I moan. "Nobody will find us until the coyotes have licked our bones clean!"

"Never mind the coyotes," Eli says, jumping right in. "We won't last the night if we don't get that fire built." He starts piling up twigs. I pick up pinecones and add them to the heap. Rosie scoops up some pine needles and sprinkles them on top. Eli rubs a couple of sticks together and makes snapping and crackling sounds. We hold our hands in front of our pretend fire. The wind whooshes through the pines, and I can almost feel the heat of the flames.

Then I hear the back door slide open. "Meena?"

Rosie starts to get up from where she's crouched down over our pile. I grab her arm and pull her back down. "Are you crazy?" I hiss. "It's a bear. Don't let it see you!"

Rosie's eyes get wide. She looks excited, but scared, too. Her eyes dart from me to Mom and back again, her cheeks pink.

"Meena!" Mom says, louder now. I can see her through the bushes, looking around the yard. She turns her head this way.

"Let's run for it," I whisper to Eli.

"What? Why?"

"Shhh!" Rosie whispers loudly. "It's a bear."

"Come on." I tug at his arm. "Now's our chance!"

"But you'll get in trouble," Eli says.

"I don't care! I just want to—" But it's too late. Mom is coming right toward us. Her steps are long and powerful. "Stay down," I hiss.

Eli ducks his head. Mom stops on the other side of our bush, puts her hands on her hips, and glares at me through the branches. "Meena," she says.

"We're lost in the woods," Rosie chirps happily. "You can't see us!"

"Meena's jacket is bright orange," she snaps. "Satellites can see her. And if you're all going to hide from me, we're leaving."

She holds out her hand. Rosie takes it and skips along, her pigtails bouncing, while Mom stalks across the yard.

Traitor.

I don't want to go home. I don't want to sit around where everything reminds me of this morning and everybody looks at me like I might burst into flames.

But Eli is squinting hard in my direction. He looks from Raymond back to me, like he has X-ray eyes that can see right through us. "That's not because you glued her keys together," he says.

I get up, brush off the pine needles, and stomp across the yard.

8

I spend the rest of the day working on coloring books with Raymond.

People are always giving me coloring books— "Since you like art," they say.

I hate coloring books. I hate how they don't give you any say in where to put the color. They just *tell* you where, and then trap it there inside the lines. Every page is like a little color prison.

So when I'm in a really bad mood, I get out a coloring book and a black pen, and I change all the pictures. I give the horses scales and fins. I draw extra arms on the princesses. I add monsters the book characters can't see in the background, coming to gobble them up.

By the time Dad calls us for dinner, I've finished redoing three whole coloring books, and I'm finally starting to feel better. I might even want to *make* something after dinner instead of just wrecking it. But as soon as we've taken our dishes to the sink, and Mom has sent Rosie to get ready for bed, she turns to me and says, "You too, Meena Zee."

I can't even believe my ears. "I have another hour," I say. "I was going to work on my box."

"Not tonight."

I look at Dad. Once in a while, when Mom tells me to do something that isn't fair, he gives me a let-me-talk-to-her wink. Then I go into the other room for a minute, and when they come in, Mom has changed her mind.

Dad doesn't wink.

I grab Raymond, stomp up the stairs, and slam the bathroom door. Mom props it open again and stands there with her arms crossed until I finish brushing my teeth. I'm so mad getting into my pajamas that at first I don't even see the thing sitting by my bed.

"What is that?" I ask, when Mom comes over. It looks like a walkie-talkie with a little blue light.

"A monitor," she says.

I remember it now! It sat by Rosie's crib when she was little. There was another one in the kitchen with a little screen so they could watch her while she slept. "That thing is for babies," I say.

"That thing is for safety," Mom replies.

"But I'm nine!"

"Meena." She presses her fingers on either side of her forehead. "You had a seizure this morning, remember?"

My jaw clamps shut. "No, I don't remember," I say through my teeth.

"Well, I do," Mom says. "And we still don't know why it happened, but I want to know if it happens again."

"So, what, you're going to *spy* on me?"

She sighs. "We're going to monitor you."

"But I'm fine!"

She opens up the covers. "I hope so."

I step back. For a second I just stand there, wringing Raymond's leg in my hands. Then I give Mom my squintiest scowl and throw myself into bed.

She pulls the blankets up over me and tries to kiss me, but I turn onto my side and make my body stiff. I hear her take a big breath and let it out. "We just want to make sure you're okay," she says.

Mom goes to tuck in Rosie. My stomach boils while they do their song about three little ducks and play This Little Piggy. I'm too old for rhymes and finger games—too old to go to bed with my little sister. I just lie there in a tight ball, turned away from them, until the last little piggy goes "wee, wee, wee."

"Mommy?" I hear Rosie say when they finish.

"Hmm?"

"What's the matter with Meena?"

I hear the bed creak as Mom sits back down.

"We don't know, sweetie," she says—like I'm not even there!

"Will someone come and take her away again?" Rosie says, her voice a squeak.

"Dad and I are going to listen closely all night long, okay? If anything happens, we'll be ready."

Rosie starts to whimper.

"Hey," Mom says. "Shhhh. . . . It was scary this morning, wasn't it?"

Rosie takes a shuddering breath. "Mm-hmm."

"There was all that shouting, and then Meena was on the floor. It was scary for all of us."

I feel my stomach crumpling up, picturing it.

"But then you know what we did?" Mom asks.

"What?"

"We did exactly the right things. What number did I call?"

"Nine-one-one," Rosie says.

"That's right. And when the ambulance came, what did you do?"

"I stayed in the corner and hugged my pony."

I picture Rosie standing in the kitchen, watching everything, and I can't help it. I want to go over and hug *her*. I squeeze Raymond tighter instead.

"Yes, you did," Mom says. "You listened so well. And when I told you to get your shoes to go to Eli's, you did it quick as a flash. And when I had to hurry off to meet Daddy at the hospital, you didn't cry or complain. You were a big helper today, Miss Rosie. Aunt Kathy said you were a big help to Eli, too."

"I got to feed Vernon," Rosie says. "And pet him."

"Oh, I bet he liked that. Do you think you might dream about playing with Vernon tonight?"

"Maybe."

"Do you think if you close your eyes, you can imagine you're petting him right now?"

"Yeah."

"Let's give it a try. Close your eyes. Now let's count. Nice and slow."

"One . . . two . . . three . . ." Rosie giggles. "His fur is soft."

"Four . . . ," Mom says, "five . . . six . . ."

Rosie keeps counting. She gets all the way up to twenty.

"Keep going," Mom whispers.

Rosie starts again. I hear the bed creak as Mom stands up. Before she leaves, she rests her hand on my back. "Good night," she says.

That's when I remember to be mad at her. I don't say good night back.

She sighs. Eventually, she heads to the door and turns out the light. I flop onto my back, kick my heel against the mattress, and glare at the ceiling. Rosie keeps counting to herself in the dark. After a while her voice gets slower and softer. She skips right over the fifties, and the sixties start to fade away. In another minute, I hear her sleep-breathing.

She sounds just like she did when I got up today.

Before everything happened.

I push up the sleeve of my pajamas and pick at the edges of the Band-Aid on the inside of my arm. This morning, at the hospital, the nurse wheeled me into a little room and had me lie still under this weird, heavy apron. Someone just outside the room stood at a control panel taking X-rays of my head. After that I thought I was done. I thought they'd give me medicine for my stomachache and let me go home.

But when we got back to the room, the nurse said they needed to test some of my blood. And it turns out the only way to do that was to take some right out of my arm with a needle.

I was not a very good sport.

It was a long time before they brought me a little pink pill for my stomach, which turned to chalk in my mouth. It was even longer before my stomach finally felt better.

I poke the Band-Aid. It still hurts under there.

I roll onto my side and hug Raymond tighter. I just want to forget this whole day—even the parts I can't remember. I don't want to imagine that anything like this could ever happen again. But I keep thinking about waking up in the hospital and the medicine smell. I keep wondering if I'll fall asleep and wake up there.

The blue light of the baby monitor is shining on me. Somewhere downstairs, Mom and Dad are listening. I know if anything happens to me, they'll hear it. They'll come running.

I'm not so mad about that anymore.

I sit up, pick up the monitor, and hold it right to my mouth.

"Good night," I say.

9

Dad is already downstairs when I wake up on Sunday. We're out of Rainbow Pops, so he makes oatmeal instead—the grayest food in the world. I kind of *wish* this stuff would end up in somebody's face, but my arms don't even bother to twitch this morning.

I don't have nearly enough color to inspire me to work on my valentine box, so Rosie and I make a school for our toys instead. I even make a clip chart. Raymond is especially good today, so I clip him all the way up to I'm Better Than You. But after I clip Pink Pony down to Now You've Done It, Rosie won't play with me anymore.

I have to do my homework before screen time.

Nobody makes green mac and cheese.

On Monday morning Dad waits for me to walk to school with him and Rosie, like I'm a little kid. It's cloudy again. The ice that looked like diamonds the other day has melted, and everything is mucky and blah.

Kindergartners have to go straight to their room while the rest of us wait outside for the bell to ring. Dad walks me all the way to the playground before he turns to take Rosie inside. "Hey," I call after him, thinking of something. I lower my voice when he turns around. "You won't tell anybody, will you? About this weekend?"

"Nobody but your teacher."

My chest squeezes. "You're telling her about my seizure?" I look around to make sure nobody can hear. "Why?"

"We need her to be part of our spy network." He winks at me and heads inside.

"Hey, Meena," Eli yells as he comes running up behind me.

"Hey," I say, plopping down on a bench.

"You wanna look for trash?" Eli asks.

I give him a hard look. On Monday mornings I look for all the beautiful trash that kids might have dropped on the playground over the weekend. But Eli usually shoots baskets with Pedro before school. "Did Aunt Kathy say you had to be nice to me?" I ask.

He shrugs. "Maybe."

"Well, you don't."

"How about I give you five minutes?" he says. "I saw some stuff under the monkey bars."

I squint at him. His ears are pink, and his freckles make him look like he's starting to rust. "What kind of things?" I ask.

"I don't know. Like a broken bracelet or something."

I make a humphy sound and kick my feet against the ground. "I don't want any more rubber bands," I say. "They don't last."

"It's not rubber bands. It's beads."

Beads? I perk right up at that. Rubber bands are for crafts, but beads are for *jewelry*!

We run for the monkey bars. A bunch of plastic beads are just sitting there on the ground! "That's enough for a whole necklace," I say. "Why would anyone leave them?"

"They probably fell in the snow," Eli says. "I bet nobody could see where they landed until it melted."

We drop to our knees and start picking them up. Every time we brush aside the wood chips, we find more beads. Some of them got trampled into the mud, and we have to dig them out with our fingers. Some are frozen in the last bits of ice, and we have to kick them loose with our heels. I grab all I can and stuff them in my pocket, breathing in the smell of the mud, feeling the wet ground soak through my jeans.

I hear a motor rumble as the bus pulls up to the school. The bell will ring any minute. I want to get every last bead before it does. I can make a new bracelet with these, but this time I'm only making one. And if anybody happens to notice me wearing it, maybe they'll wonder if I gave a matching one to some new best friend they don't know about. Maybe they'll remember that *I'm* not the one who started staying in every recess.

I'm the one who kept playing and swinging and looking for beautiful trash, even when I had to do it alone.

I almost have all the colors now. If I can just find a yellow one, I'll have every color in the rainbow!

The bell rings. Eli gets up off the ground. All around us, kids start running for the door.

I see a yellow bead! There, in a chunk of ice. I try to pick it up, but it's frozen to the ground. I pound my fist against it, but it doesn't come loose.

"Are you coming?" Eli asks.

I look over my shoulder. The grades are lining up by the door. "Just a second," I say. I stand up and start hammering the ice with my heel. *Whack! Whack! Whack!*

"Meena—"

The playground monitor starts calling classes inside. "First grade!"

"I've almost got it."

"Second grade!"

"We're gonna get in trouble."

"Third grade!"

"You go. I'm coming."

Eli hangs back for a few seconds, then hurries toward the school.

I switch to the other heel.

"Fourth grade!"

Whack! Whack!

"Fifth grade!"

Crack! The ice chunk breaks loose. The yellow bead is frozen in the middle of the hunk, so I jam the whole thing into the pocket of my hoodie, grab my backpack, and run for the door.

The playground is empty now. The last of the fifth graders have disappeared inside. The monitor is leaning against the open door with her arms crossed. "Better get a move on," she says.

I hurry down the hall. Kids have hung things up in their cubbies and are heading into their classrooms. My jeans are soaked, and mud falls in clumps off my shoes, leaving a chunky trail behind me. But my pockets are full of rainbows, and the ice makes a nice solid *thunk* against my stomach. I round the last corner. Maybe if I walk just a little bit faster, I can make it to class before—

The late bell rings.

Mrs. D is standing by our door.

I stop in my tracks. She'll clip me down for this. Mrs. D is a pretty nice teacher and all, but she does *not* believe in rainbow emergencies. She heads toward me. Her forehead wrinkles. She looks down at my shoes, and her mouth forms a thin line.

Then something weird happens. She looks me right in the eye and gives me her first-day-of-school smile. "I'm so glad you're here, Meena," she says in a shiny voice. "Why don't you just leave your shoes in the hall before you join us."

She knows.

She waits while I unpack my things and pull off my sneakers. My face heats up, and the skin on my arms gets that prickly, spied-on feeling. I duck my head and slip past her into the room.

I keep my head down when I get to my desk and take out my homework. Lin is going around collecting worksheets. She must be the Homework Handler this week. Aiden is whizzing pencils through the sharpener, so I guess he's the Pencil Police.

Everyone gets a new classroom job on Mondays. They're nothing to get excited about. My last job was Line Leader. But it turns out even in third grade you don't really lead the line. You're just the first to follow the teacher. And when you try to pass, she says your name in a stern voice and tells you there's no running in the hall.

When we're all in our seats, Mrs. D says, "Raise

your hand if you're eating school lunch today." Only a few kids put their hands in the air, because it's creamed turkey day. She writes a number down on a slip of paper. "Who's taking this to the office?"

I check the jobs board, and it's me! I'm Lunch Patrol! I've been waiting all year to do that job. It's the only good one. You get to go around to every single classroom and collect all the lunch slips for the office *all by yourself.* That job doesn't even *exist* until you're in third grade, because I mean, would you trust second graders to wander around the school without a teacher?

And I get to do it in my socks!

I hurry over to Mrs. D. She starts to hand me the slip, but at the last second she doesn't let go. "Um, Mrs. D," I say, "I can take it from here."

Now she's starting to chew her bottom lip. She looks just like Mom and Dad did when they were peeking through the doorways at me. She grips the slip tighter and peeks over my shoulder. "Who did Lunch Patrol last week?" she asks.

Oh, no. No, no, no.

Sofía raises her hand. Her flower headband is blue today.

"Would you go along with Meena, please?" Mrs. D says.

Sofía jumps up. When she smiles, I see new rubber bands on her braces. They're all different colors now. She already had the only good job in the class last week, and now she gets to do it *again*?

I grit my stupid, straight teeth. If I can't have braces, I wish I could at least color over the white. Only it turns out markers don't stick to teeth. They just turn the inside of your mouth purple—even *permanent* markers, which is false advertising I think.

I turn back to Mrs. D. "I can do it myself," I say.

She gives my arm a pat. "Just let Sofía show you the ropes, okay?" She lets go of the slip.

I don't need Sofía to show me any ropes. And I don't need Mrs. D sending her to spy on me! I spin around and stomp into the hall.

"Not so fast," I hear Sofía say.

But I am not slowing down. I would have waited for the Sofía who smeared paint and made me a bracelet and launched herself off the top of the swings when the playground monitor wasn't looking.

But *this* Sofía stopped playing with me after *three years together.* This Sofía has to be the best at everything, no matter who she leaves behind.

So if she thinks I'm waiting for her now, she's crazy.

She catches up anyway, halfway to the fifth-grade room. "Did you get in trouble or something?" she asks.

I don't look at her. I just say, "No." My voice

sounds like a rubber band stretched tight.

"Then how come Mrs. D won't let you go by yourself?"

"How should I know?"

The door of the fifth-grade room is closed when we get there. I look through the window and see the teacher at the board. "So, the first thing we do—" Sofía says.

She's not the boss of me. I push open the door and walk right in. "I'm here for the lunch count," I say, sticking my chin out.

The teacher sighs and lowers his dry-erase maker. "It's taped to the door," he says. "So you don't have to interrupt my class."

"Oh," I say. "Got it. Sorry." I back out of there and quietly pull the door closed behind me. I check for the slip.

Sofía is already holding it.

I glare at her and head back down the hall. I stomp to the fourth-grade room and check the door. It's standing wide open, and there's nothing taped to it, but I don't know if I'm supposed to barge in. Sofía is catching up! I start clearing my throat until the teacher notices me, walks over—

—and hands the slip to Sofía!

Are you kidding me? Now Sofía has two of them!

No way is she getting any more. I may not be

good at spelling, and I may lose my homework inside my own backpack sometimes, but I can collect the dumb lunch slips.

She starts heading to second grade without me. I hurry in front of her, the ice in my hoodie pocket thumping against my stomach. "You're not Line Leader, too," I say over my shoulder. I rush past the third-grade room. I notice Mrs. D hung our President Portraits across the hall, but I don't have time to stop and look at those—and I don't want to see my scribbled-on picture anyway. I walk right up to the second-grade door. I knock nice and loud, then run right in and get the slip.

Now I have two. I'm tied with Sofía!

When I get to first grade, I don't even knock. The teacher looks at me like she's kind of annoyed, but I don't care. It's three to two. Now if I can just get the kindergarten slip, I'll win. I hurry to the last door and see the kids all sitting in a circle on the rug, singing. I reach for the handle.

"Meena, wait," Sofía whispers loudly behind me.

I burst through the door. The kids stop singing and look up. I spot Rosie and give her a little wave. She's so excited to see me that she actually jumps up, runs over, and almost plows me over. "Hey, squirt," I whisper, giving her a quick hug and shooing her back to the rug.

Her teacher is sitting cross-legged on the floor

with the other kids. "What's up, Meena?" he asks, tilting his head at me.

I stand straight and tall. "I'm here for the lunch count," I say, looking right at Rosie. She's never even *seen* me do this job before!

But she just blinks and looks at her teacher.

"This class doesn't stay for lunch," he says. "They're only here for the morning, remember?"

"Oh!" I feel my cheeks getting hot. "Right." Rosie looks from me to her teacher and back again, crinkling her forehead. I shift between my feet. "How about the milk count? You need any help with that?"

"We're all set, thanks."

The little girl next to Rosie starts to giggle. Rosie elbows her in the side.

"Hands to yourself, please," the teacher says.

I walk backward into the hall. I feel the ice melting through my pocket as I ease the door shut. The last thing I see is the sorry look on Rosie's face.

When I turn around, Sofía has her hands on her hips. "I tried to tell you," she says. "Come on." She reaches over and grabs the slips out of my hand. "I'll show you how to take them to the office."

I glare at the back of her head, her blue flower bobbing as she walks away.

But I don't say anything. I just reach into my pocket, grab hold of my icy chunk, and follow her.

The rest of the day, Mrs. D sends spies with me everywhere I go. She even has girls take turns walking me to the bathroom!

I'm so sick of everybody following me around that I accidentally forget to come in when the bell rings after recess. I just lie down by myself inside the big tube slide all alone, breathing in the plastic air and trying to soak up the feeling of being surrounded by orange.

I only stay in there for a couple of extra minutes. How am I supposed to know they lock the playground doors behind everybody, and by the time you walk around the whole building and get buzzed in the front entrance, they're already so freaked out that you're gone that they call a code yellow over the loudspeakers and even the *janitor* is looking for you?

I get clipped down to Think About Your Choices for that.

Then later, when I'm making my rain-forest

diorama, I get into a tug-of-war with Lin over the green paint, and one of us ends up with splatters all over her clothes.

Turns out it's me.

Why did she need green paint for her ocean anyway? Those dumb fish could have been any color.

I get clipped all the way down to Last Chance—just one away from Go to the Principal, and nobody's gotten that since Aiden taught some first graders to swear!

It takes me all afternoon to clip back up. I have to make sure Mrs. D sees me helping Pedro pick up the papers he dropped *and* giving Nora the fuzzy beanbag chair at reading time, even though I totally had it first.

But at the end of the day, my clothespin is right back where it started. Sofía's is at the top, like always. *She* never ignores the bell or forgets the rules about sharing. Just looking at Sofía's clip makes me write my spelling words all crooked.

Mrs. D says Ready for Anything is a fine place to be. She says it means you're doing what you're supposed to.

I think it might as well say Nothing Special.

I squirm in my desk while I finish my words. I wish I could just go home and work on my valentine box. The clock ticks closer to three. But the bell keeps not ringing. I keep wriggling.

Then finally we're closing our notebooks, and Mrs. D is saying, "Don't forget, tomorrow is our one hundredth day of school."

Well, *that* makes me feel springy again! My hand shoots up in the air and starts waving. "Can we do crazy hair again this year?"

"You bet," says Mrs. D. "And we'll run a hundred-meter dash and try hula-hooping to one hundred, and we'll eat a hundred M&M's for a special snack."

Finally, stuff I'm good at!

"What do you get if your hair is the craziest?" I ask.

"You don't get anything, Meena. It's not a contest."

I peek over at Sofía and her blue-flower head. At least I can make my hair crazier than hers. It will be the craziest in our whole class.

As soon as the bell rings, I dart out of there—away from my halfway-there clip and my not-good-enough writing and all the spies that follow me. I wave to Eli and race out of the building. I'm going to make this the longest, daydreamiest walk ever. I'll think up something awesome for my hair while I look for beautiful trash. Maybe I'll find new colors for my twist-tie collection or one of those red nets that oranges come in. Maybe I'll find something so beautiful that it will spark a brilliant idea for my valentine box, and I'll have to run the rest of the way home to work on it.

Only, I don't get to find anything because just as I'm skipping past the parking lot, I hear someone calling my name.

I turn toward the sound. Mom is standing by our car, waving.

The happiness leaks right out through my toes. I scuff my feet over to her. "What are you doing here?" I ask.

"Taking you to the doctor," she says.

My whole body wilts like lunchroom lettuce. "I was going to look for trash."

Mom opens the car door. "Sorry, hon. We were lucky to get you in." She looks me up and down. "What happened to you?"

I forgot about the green paint.

Oh, and the mud.

Dad is already in the front when I climb in. "What's the word, hummingbird?" he says.

I slump in my seat.

"Everything go okay today?"

I scowl. "I got clipped down again."

"Something to do with your clothes, I'm guessing." He turns all the way around and looks at me with a very serious expression. "So where are you now? Cruisin' for a Bruisin'?"

I smile a little.

"Put Me on the Curb?"

"Dad."

He points a finger, but his eyes are twinkling. "You'd better watch yourself, young lady. Sounds like you're On a Ski Run to Smackdown."

Dr. Suri smiles at me when she comes into our little exam room.

At least one of us is happy to be here.

Last time I saw her, she was totally taking Mom's side on the more-vegetables-less-screen-time thing, but I'm trying not to hold that against her.

"I hear you had some excitement over the weekend," she says.

I kick my heels against the exam table while Mom and Dad tell her about my seizure. I start out listening, but then I get distracted thinking about what I could do with those jars of cotton balls and tongue depressors. Plus, I can't stop looking at the bright red liner in the garbage can. I wonder where you even *get* trash bags that color.

When they're finished, Dr. Suri turns to me. "Mind if I check you over?" she says.

I shrug. She shines a light in my eyes and ears. "What does that tell you?" I ask.

"That you don't eat enough dark leafy greens," Dad says.

She feels the sides of my neck.

"That tells her you leave your socks all over the house," Dad adds.

I grin. "I get hot feet."

She taps a little hammer on my elbows and knees.

Dad leans closer. "Now she knows you forget to flush."

"Dad!"

I'm still giggling when Dr. Suri says, "Okay, you can hop down." I go and punch Dad on the arm while the doctor brings up a picture on a screen. "So here's what I can tell you," she says, turning the screen to us. "This is from the CT scan they did at the hospital."

I stop laughing. It's an X-ray of a skull. *My* skull.

Dad nudges my shoulder. "Check it out. That's pretty cool, huh?"

But it isn't cool. It's creepy. Looking at it makes me think of dead people. It makes me think about *being* a dead person. It makes me want to climb onto somebody's lap, only I'm nine, so I don't. Instead I take a step back and put my hand over the pocket of my jeans to make sure my beads are still there.

The doctor points to a blurry white smudge at the edge of the picture. Then she touches her finger to the top of my head and lets it rest there. "This is the spot we're looking at," she says. "Right about here."

Her hand is warm, but a little shiver ripples down from the place she's touching. When she moves her hand away, I reach up to feel for myself.

There's nothing there. It's just hair and a dried-up splatter of green paint. "I don't feel anything," I say.

"That's because it's on the inside."

Nobody says anything. I hear the clock on the wall.

Tick. Tick. Tick.

Mom clears her throat. "What is it?" she asks. Her voice is almost a squeak.

"It might be nothing," Dr. Suri says. She's quiet for a few *ticks*. She looks from Mom to Dad and back again but not at me. "Or it might be something else."

I start to feel shaky. I turn and stare at that white shadow in the X-ray. How did I get something in my head? The doctor starts talking again, but I can't hear what she's saying because there's a rushing sound in my ears and my throat is closing. I reach into the deepest part of my pocket, grab a fistful of beads, and squeeze them so tight that I can feel them making dents in my skin.

My heart is pounding through to my fingers. And I do climb onto Mom's lap. Even though I'm nine.

"Do you understand what Dr. Suri is telling us?" Mom finally asks.

I take a gulp of air and shake my head.

"She says lots of people have spots like this." Mom starts stroking my hair. "She says it could just be the regular shape of your skull. It might not be a problem at all. But if it isn't—" She stops.

Everyone is quiet. Nobody says if it isn't . . . *what*?

The rushing sound in my ears gets louder. My face feels hot. My hands feel cold.

The spot isn't nothing. It can't be. It gave me a seizure, didn't it? *Something* makes my arms herky and jerky in the morning. *Something* made me dizzy from the flashing lights.

So it's something. In my head. It must be.

My teeth start to chatter. Dad leans in close. "We're going to do some tests," he says, "to see if that spot is a normal part of your skull."

Tears start to form in the back of my eyes. "Or if it's something else," I say.

He starts rubbing my back. "We've got you, honey," Mom says. "We're going to figure this out, okay?" She presses her head against mine.

I nod and take a shuddery breath. I try to concentrate my whole body on keeping the tears inside.

"What kind of tests?" I say.

11

We're all pretty quiet at dinner. Even though it's taco night.

Rosie is the only one talking. She stayed at Eli's again while we went to the doctor. This time they set up blocks like bowling pins and watched Vernon knock them over.

She's pretty chatty about it.

Usually I pile everything so high that my tortilla explodes when I try to close it, and I end up having to eat it with a fork, which is not even fair, because tacos are finger food.

But I don't think I can fit an explosion of taco inside me tonight. Not with how small my stomach feels. I sprinkle some cheese onto a tortilla and roll it up.

"You want some salsa with that?" Dad asks.

I shake my head.

"How about a slather of guacamole? Green things up a bit?"

I pick up my tight little roll and nibble at the end.

I watch Dad drop a blob of sour cream onto his taco salad. It makes me think of the blurry white spot on the X-ray.

The bite of taco sticks in my throat. I have to swallow hard to get it down.

I don't want to think about skulls and doctors and white smudges.

So I think about my valentine box.

It doesn't matter if I'm in the mood to work on it. My box isn't even close to finished. It has to be bigger. It has to be better. It has to beat Sofía.

And I'm running out of time.

As soon as we clear the table, I get my math homework over with and spread out my art supplies. Next I dig into my pockets and dump my new beads onto the table. They're still muddy, but they might give me an Inspiration anyway. I prop Raymond up next to me so he can watch me work, then I look through the recycling bin and pull out some tomato cans. I rinse them and tear off the labels. When I set my box on top of the cans, they look a little bit like legs.

I start gluing candy wrappers onto them to match the rest of my box. After her bath, Rosie comes and leans on her elbows beside me. Her hair is wet and smells like coconut. "Now what are you making?" she asks.

I shrug. "I'm not sure."

"It looks like it's breathing," she says.

I stop and look. The foil wrappers shimmer under the light. When I tilt my head to the side, the light shimmies over the top in a way that makes it look like the *box* is moving—like it's taking a big breath in. When I tilt my head the other way, it looks like it's letting the big breath out.

I smile at Rosie. "You want to hand me a gold wrapper?" She sets Pink Pony on the table, reaches into the pile, and pulls one out. "I need a red one next," I say. "Then a silver one."

She climbs up into the chair next to me and starts kicking her feet against the legs. Mom and Dad are washing the dishes at the sink. They're leaning their heads close together, whispering.

I bet they're talking about me. I don't want to hear what they're saying. I concentrate on the crinkling sound the wrappers make. I try to listen to the little tune Rosie is always humming to herself.

"Meena?" she says, handing me the next wrapper.

"Hmm?"

"Are you going to have another seizure?"

I freeze. Did she really just ask me that? "I

don't know," I say, my stomach tightening.

"Will you have to ride in the am-blee-ance again?"

Now I'm thinking of the muddy tracks on the floor and getting that ocean sound in my ears. "I don't know," I say again through clenched teeth.

"Will you have to go back to the hospital?"

I jump off my chair. "I don't *know*, Rosie!" I'm yelling now, grabbing my hair. "Stop talking about it!"

She starts to cry. "Hey!" Mom drops the dish towel and comes over. She wraps Rosie up in a hug. "What's going on?"

I shove my chair toward the table. "Make her stop asking me," I yell.

"She's just worried about you, Meena."

She is. I know she is. But *I'm* worried about me too! I can't get enough air, and there's so much noise that I cover my ears, only I can still hear everything—the ocean crashing and Rosie crying— and the next thing I know my fingers are climbing up and feeling around my head, and I imagine another sound, too—my doctor's voice. *This is the spot. Right about here.*

Then another sound breaks through, louder than all the rest. It's clapping. It's Dad making three big claps in the air.

"Come on," he says. "Into the living room, everybody. It's story time."

He puts his hands on my shoulders and steers me into the other room. I slump into the middle of the couch and hug my knees to my chest.

We haven't read stories together this whole year—not since I started third grade and said I was too big for it. But we all go straight for our old spots. Mom sits next to me with Rosie in her lap. Rosie buries her face in Mom's shoulder and whimpers. Dad grabs our big, blue Winnie the Pooh book from the shelf and squeezes in on my other side. He doesn't even ask what story. He just turns right to the one where Pooh tries to steal honey from some bees.

"Once upon a time," Dad says, "a very long time ago now, about last Friday . . ." At first that's all I hear. I'm curled up into a ball that's too small and too tight to let in anything else, so his words just flutter down like leaves and land in a soft pile on top of me.

My grip around my legs loosens. My chest starts to let in more air, and the steady sound of Dad's voice gathers into words. When Pooh falls in a gorse-bush and Rosie leans in to look at the pictures, I rest my head against hers. When Pooh rolls around in the mud to look like a storm cloud, Mom reaches for my hand. When Pooh grabs hold of a balloon and floats up into the tree, Dad puts his arm around me.

For a little while, everything feels just like it's supposed to. I keep that feeling tucked up inside all the way to the end of the next story. When Mom carries Rosie up to bed, I get Pink Pony from the kitchen and set her next to Rosie's head on the pillow. I smooth out Pink Pony's mane. I smooth Rosie's hair. Then I slip under my own covers.

It's not until I'm lying there in the dark, listening to Rosie sleep-breathe, that I remember the white spot on the X-ray again. I hold on tight to Raymond and try to think about other things. Like my valentine box. Or about what kind of crazy hair I'll do tomorrow. But I can't get my mind to stick there. Every time I start to feel sleepy, Rosie's questions pop into my head and wake me right back up.

Are you going to have another seizure?

Will you have to ride in the ambulance again?

Will you have to go back to the hospital?

Each question zaps like a shock to my chest— like when I'm making popcorn and the first kernel bursts, then another, and then a bunch of them at once. And pretty soon the bag is filling up and turning and steaming until it just can't hold another single piece.

When my body is too full for one more scary thought inside me, I creep down the stairs.

Mom and Dad are sitting at the kitchen table

with their hands folded, like they're waiting for something. I can hear Rosie breathing loud and clear through the baby monitor on the counter. I look over and see my empty bed on the screen, and I realize that they must have seen me coming. They're waiting for me.

"What's up, honey?" Mom says.

I shift back and forth on my feet. "Will I have another seizure?" I ask them.

Dad reaches over and crooks his finger around my pinky. "We don't know," he says.

"What if I do?"

"Then we'll deal with it together," Mom says. "We'll do whatever we can to keep you safe. Okay?"

I squeeze my eyes shut and nod. I want that to be enough. It's just . . . what if there are things they *can't* do? Things nobody can?

"Come on," Dad says, standing up. "Let's get you back to bed."

We go up the stairs again. He lifts up the covers for me. I climb back in.

"You want me to stay for a while?" he asks.

I can't think of anything more babyish than having someone stay with me while I fall asleep. But I let out a big breath and nod.

Dad tucks the blankets in around me. Then he sits on the edge of my bed and starts to whisper-sing like he did every night, back when I still let

people sing to me. I fill in the last word of every line, just like before, when I used to sing along.

"There was a little—"

"—girl—"

"—and she had a little—"

"—curl—"

"—right in the middle of her—"

"—forehead."

"And when she was—"

"—good—"

"—she was very, very—"

"—good."

"And when she was bad, she was—"

"—horrid."

The bed feels softer now. The blankets feel fluffier. As long as Dad stays beside me, nothing seems as scary. I turn onto my side with Raymond and think about clouds and honey and rolling in the mud. Soon my mind is just a swirl of color, turning like a pinwheel. And the last thing I know, I'm drifting. I'm floating into the air, like when the big balloon carries Winnie the Pooh up, up, and away.

The next morning I wake up to a rainbow.

The sun is shining through ice crystals on the outside of my window, making a kaleidoscope prism on the wall above. The black X-ray with the white smudge feels like something out of a dream now, not part of this bright morning where nothing bad has happened or ever could, like someone took a big pitcher of courage and filled me up to the top.

I feel like I can make the craziest hair in the world!

I leap out of bed, throw on my clothes, and pull my tie-dyed hoodie on over them. Then I grab Raymond and hurry to my workshop. I stop long enough to draw a girl with crazy hair in the Magic Mist. I make a wish that my hair will be the craziest in the class, because who says you can't wish on windows? Then I grab some of my hair accessories, head into the bathroom, and study my face in the mirror, waiting for Inspiration.

Clips or pigtails?

I set Raymond on the sink and try pigtails first. I make seven of them sticking out all over my head. Once or twice, my hands do that herky-jerky thing, but I am *not* going to let that bother me. Besides, it actually makes the pigtails even more crooked. When I'm done, my hair looks okay, but not good enough. I did use all different colors of rubber bands, but I use them even for regular hair days, and this has to be the *craziest*.

I take everything out and start over. This time I hold up a piece of hair and drag a comb the wrong way through it. My hair gets all bunched up and knotted. Then I take another piece and another. Once my hand yanks so hard that I pull my own hair and make a little yelp.

"Meena?" Mom says, knocking on the door. "Are you okay?"

I rub the sore spot with my fingers. "I'll be out in a sec," I say. I comb the last piece of hair backward and check myself out in the mirror. My hair is all clumps and frizzy ends, like a big mop of static cling. It still needs something else. I grab all different colored pipe cleaners and twist them into my hair so they're springing out everywhere.

Now *this* is crazy hair. I grin at myself in the mirror. Even Raymond looks like he approves, and he already has the craziest rainbow-striped fur in the world.

When I head into the kitchen, I see that Mom put Rosie's hair in crooked pigtails with different-colored rubber bands. So that was a close one! Rosie gasps when she sees me, just like I hoped she would. "You're like a rainbow," she says, bouncing in her chair.

Mom looks up from pouring juice and sighs.

"What do you think?" I ask.

"It's crazy all right," she says. "But you're on your own combing it out later."

Just then Dad comes in the door wearing his scuba running suit. He lights up when he sees me, but when he sees the look Mom is making, he puts on a sort of twinkly frown instead. "What's up, buttercup?" he says.

I do a happy twirl for him.

"Something's different about you today," he says, rubbing his chin. "I can't put my finger on it."

"Her hair," Rosie squeals, clapping. "It's her hair!"

"Oh, *now* I see," Dad says. He walks around me. "Yes, it looks like very delicate work."

I start bouncing on my toes. It *is* the craziest. I just know it. There's no way Sofía can beat this!

"Do you think I'll win the prize for Crazy Hair Day?" I ask.

He laughs. "If Crazy Hair Day were actually a contest," he says, "and there were actually a prize, I don't see how you could lose."

I see a lot of crazy hair when Dad drops me off at the playground. I see slicked-back and spiky styles. I see pigtails sprouting like fountains. I see kids who look like they just didn't bother to brush.

But a lot of people turn to look at me.

"Wow, your hair!" Eli yells, running up. He's got his slicked back on top and spiked out at the sides. He reaches over to feel my head. When he pulls away, the staticky ends stick to his hand like magnets. Other kids start touching my hair too. Pretty soon hands are reaching for my head from every side.

I can't wait for Sofía to see me! I scan the area and spot her mom walking away, so Sofía must be here somewhere. I adjust the pipe cleaners to make sure they're at their pointiest and stretch up on my tiptoes.

There she is! Sofía's heading for the playground! She's still kind of far away, but even from here, I can tell that her hair is braided into two long ropes that curve out to the side and up over her head. When she gets a little closer, I see that they join together in the shape of a heart. The whole thing is sprayed with something red and glittery and makes her about a foot taller!

"Look at Sofía," somebody yells. The heads around me all turn. Then everybody is running over, huddling around Sofía, touching *her* hair and gasping. "How did you get it to do that?" someone asks.

Sofía touches her sparkly heart hair. "I used a coat hanger," she says.

A coat hanger! Why didn't I think of that?

I sink down onto a bench and watch everyone swarm her. When the bell finally rings, I scuff my feet down the hallway and shove everything into my cubby. I slump in my desk and cross my arms tight across my chest. When Lin comes by and picks up my spelling homework, she shakes her head. Her short hair is spiked with so much gel that it doesn't even move.

"Mrs. D will make you do this over," she says. "We're not supposed to do anything in print anymore."

I groan and put my head down. Just because we're learning stupid cursive this year, Mrs. D wants us to use it all the time now. But what's wrong with printing? Maybe my letters don't *want* to join up with the others. Maybe they're not interested in blending together with every other letter in the world. Did anybody ever think of that? Maybe they want to be left alone. And just because they stuck together at the start of third grade doesn't mean they will forever.

I grab my homework back from Lin and cram it into my desk. I am *not* getting clipped down for printing. And I won't give up on winning Crazy Hair Day, either. I didn't spend ninety-nine days in third grade just to lose to a dumb coat hanger! So while Mrs. D starts counting hands for lunch and Lin puts our homework in the basket and Aiden finishes sharpening pencils, I walk very casually to the tissue box in the corner. I pretend to blow my nose. Then, when no one is looking, I grab what I need from the art cart and slip it into the front pouch of my hoodie.

I'm just getting back to my desk when Mrs. D holds out the lunch slip. "Here you go, girls," she says. I grab it from her and head out of the room.

As soon as we're in the hall, I turn and hand Sofía the slip. "Here," I say. "You do it."

I do not say anything about her hair. Not. One. Word.

Which is actually pretty hard. Because it looks amazing.

She blinks at me and frowns. "We're supposed to stay together," she says.

Like she knows anything about staying together.

"I'm just going to the bathroom," I say. "Can't anybody even pee by themselves around here anymore?"

I spin around and hurry into the closest bathroom. For a second I'm afraid she's going to follow me, but she doesn't.

So I get to work.

It's harder than I expected. I know I only have a few minutes, and my hair doesn't exactly cooperate now that it's brushed in all different directions. But I manage to get it pretty close to how I want it to look. When I'm finished, I turn upside down and fluff out the hair one last time.

"Meena?" I hear Sofía say from the hall. "Are you okay in there?"

I am *awesome* in here.

When I step out of the bathroom, Sofía puts a hand over her mouth.

That seems like a good sign.

We walk back into the room. Now I'm the one who feels taller. It's super quiet since everyone is working on their language arts journals while Mrs. D writes something on the board. Sofía slips back into her desk. I plop down and clear my throat. When nobody looks, I bump my knee against Eli's.

He looks up at me and knocks his journal on the floor. "Is that *marker*?" he says.

Finally, everyone turns to look.

I flip my hair off my shoulder. "It's rainbow highlights," I say.

Some kids gasp. Some laugh. A few even jump out of their desks to get a closer look.

"Class—" Mrs. D starts to say.

I shake my hair and turn my head so everyone can see how the streaks go all the way around. I made sure the red and orange and yellow stripes in front stretch from my forehead to the ends of my hair. I'm pretty sure the green and blue and purple streaks do, too, but it was hard coloring them on the back of my head.

Then I look at Mrs. D. She doesn't say anything. She just gazes back at me with a wrinkled brow.

I bet she's deciding on a prize for Crazy Hair Day!

Except then she squeezes her eyes shut and cradles her forehead. "Meena," she says, "did you use permanent marker to do that?"

Well, duh. "I wanted it to last," I say.

Her shoulders slump. She sighs.

When Mrs. D. finally opens her eyes, all she says is, "Take out your free reading books, please. Group B, meet me at the table."

Mrs. D goes over to the behavior chart and moves my clothespin down.

I stare at my clip. It's the first one down today. It's just sitting there below all the others now, at Think About Your Choices.

But I *did* think about my choices! I thought about how I could beat Sofía at Crazy Hair Day. And I did! Didn't I?

I glance at Sofía. She only looks back for a second before her eyes drop down to her desk.

And after that the one hundredth day of school ends up being a big, huge flop.

I don't win Crazy Hair Day.

I can only hula-hoop to twelve.

And it turns out the whole class has to share a hundred M&M's!

Trust me. That's way less chocolate than you think.

My rainbow highlights fade a little when I wash my hair the next morning, but the guy at the hospital can still see them. "Is that a thing now?" he asks. "Kids coloring their hair?"

I glance at Mom. She doesn't answer but just crosses her arms, raises an eyebrow, and waits for me to speak. She's not as mad about my hair as she was yesterday, but she's not going to help me out here either.

I shrug at the guy. "It's *my* thing," I say.

"Got it," he replies. He pats a table-bed that's sticking out of a white machine. "Hop on up here for me, would you?"

I didn't wake up in the hospital this time. I came back so they could take more pictures of my brain. This time they're using an MRI machine. That stands for Magnetic Something Something.

A shiver curls down my spine just looking at that thing. It's like a giant washing machine from the future. It even says GE on the front, like the one in our laundry room. I hold tighter to Raymond. "Can I bring my zebra?" I ask.

The guy looks at Mom.

"No metals," she says. "I even took the grommets off her hoodie."

He smiles at me. "Zebras welcome. All aboard."

I pull up the hood of my tie-dyed sweatshirt, tighten the strings so it closes around my head, and climb up onto the table.

Before we came this morning, I painted my nails all different colors and took my time picking out socks that didn't match. I ate two bowls of Rainbow Pops and made sure to put on my shoes with the colorful laces. But now, even covered with my rainbow armor, I feel wimpy and small next to this big white machine.

Mom helps me squish in these little foam earplugs. They fill up the empty space in my ears and make everything sound muffled. The guy gives me a pair of headphones and then goes into a little room behind a window. I see him talk into a microphone and hear his voice through the headphones, right through the earplugs. "I need you to be perfectly still in there, okay?" he says.

I nod.

"Go ahead and lie down."

The table starts to move me backward into the machine. It's smooth and round and cramped in here, like the tube slide at school, only white. Music starts playing through the headphones: "The Wheels on the Bus."

I roll my eyes, even though I'm not supposed to move. What does he think I am, *five*?

The machine starts to whir and hum. Something inside the machine goes *BANG*, and I flinch. Banging sounds fire up all around me. Even with foam in my ears, it's as loud as when Rosie used to drum on our pots and pans. But I stay still. I don't cover my ears. I try not to blink. I'm not sure I even breathe. Only my toes are twitching, sticking out of the machine. Mom is out there too—a million miles away. She puts her hand on my leg. I want to reach out and grab her hand. I want to squeeze Raymond tighter.

But I don't move.

And then, just when the music ends and I think I'm finally getting away from this thing, the song starts right back at the beginning—and so does the banging. The lyrics play over and over while I lie there, frozen, bombarded by colorless noise.

I wish I were in my workshop, where nothing is clean, and it smells like glue, and I can reach my arms out and twirl around. But it seems like I'm in here forever with the machine banging and the wheels turning, until finally everything stops.

The table starts to slide out of the tube. I take

a big breath and open and close my eyes a bunch of times to fill up on blinks.

"You're doing great, Meena," the guy says. "We just need one more set of pictures." He's standing by the table now.

And he's holding a needle.

A numbing sensation floods my whole body. I don't say anything at first. When I do ask him, "What's that for?" my voice sounds calm and quiet.

"It's for contrast," he says. "It will make your blood vessels show up better in the pictures."

Mom looks at me with wide eyes. She looks back at the guy. "I told her it wasn't that kind of a test," she says. "I told her she wouldn't need one."

He lowers the syringe. His eyebrows scrunch together as he looks from Mom to me, then back at Mom again.

He looks sorry. But all he says is, "She does."

"You want to go somewhere for lunch?" Mom asks when we're driving home.

I'm not hungry at all. I lean my head against the window and cradle my arm where it's still sore from the shot.

She reaches over and strokes my hair. "Then how about we make a quick stop at the art store?" Mom says. "You can pick out some new paints. Or that air-dry clay you like."

I shake my head and keep my eyes on the thin, streaky clouds out my window. I just want to go home.

When we finally pull into the driveway, Mom parks right over the little spill of oil, so I can't even see the rainbow splotch when I get out. Dad is waiting for us in the kitchen. He scrapes his chair back from the table and holds his arms open for me. "There she is," he says.

I don't even take off my coat or kick off my shoes. I just shuffle over and slump against him.

"What's the tale, nightingale?" he asks quietly, hugging me.

I swallow. "I had to get a shot."

"Ah," he says. "Not your favorite."

"Not my favorite."

My body goes slack inside his hug. I'd let him pick me up and carry me if it meant I didn't have to hold myself up anymore. I used all my energy on the guy at the hospital. It's not like I meant to fight him. I didn't mean to kick him or bat at his arms or shout "Wait a minute!" over and over until he finally called someone to hold me while he gave me the shot. I didn't mean to cry. And I definitely don't mean to start crying *again* now, when it's over and done with, but the next thing I know I'm snuffling and Dad's shirt is getting wet.

"It's not fair," I mutter into him. "Why is this happening?"

He rubs my back and kisses the top of my head. "I don't know," he says. "Maybe it's just your turn. Everybody has tough times, Meena."

"*Every*body?" I ask.

"Sure. We all have ups and downs."

I *humph* at that, because it reminds me of the clip chart at school. I picture my clothespin and how it's always moving down, while Sofía's shoots up to the top. "It seems like some people have nothing but Ups," I say.

I wonder when it's Sofía's turn for a Down. And just like that, I know I can't stand going to class and watching our clips going in opposite directions. I step back from Dad and dry the rest of my tears with my sleeve. "I think I'll just stay home from school today."

He ruffles my hair. "Nice try."

I groan. "I've been through kind of an ordeal here, you know."

"Oh, really?" he says, grabbing my backpack from its hook. He zips my lunch bag inside and gives Mom a grin. "Then I guess beating you there will be a cinch," he says.

I stop sniffling and look him over. He's usually faster than me, but he's not wearing his running gear today. He's in his work clothes with those stiff, heavy shoes.

And I have on sneakers with rainbow laces.

I feel just the tiniest bit of a smile coming on before I run for the door.

"It's Meena with an early lead!" Dad yells from behind. I hear the door smack shut and feel a cold breeze slap my face. I shoot down our driveway and veer onto the sidewalk. Dad is close. The edge of his shadow falls over me, and I pump my arms and legs harder.

"Dad is bringing up the rear," he calls, "but he's still the odds-on favorite in this race. Wait! Don't look now! He's coming alive!"

He pulls up next to me. I hear my backpack thumping on his shoulder and his shoes clomping down the sidewalk. For half a block, he takes the lead. I pound my feet harder, propelling my body forward, the cold air stinging inside my chest, until I edge past him again.

My hair is flying behind me. My cheeks are getting numb. When we round the last corner to school, my side starts to hurt. I can't get enough air. I start to fall back, and Dad grazes my shoulder as he passes me.

"They're at the top of the stretch now, folks," he says. "It looks like Meena is done for. Dad has this win in the bag!"

I am not finished yet! My side feels like it's splitting in half, but I bite down on my lip, take a big breath, and push myself even harder.

"What's this? Meena isn't out of it! She's coming from behind!"

I see the swing set in the distance. Dad heads for the pavement, but I take a chance and cut through the soccer field. The ground isn't mucky today. It's cold, and I stumble over the frozen ridges of mud. If I can just stay on my feet, I'll win this thing!

I'm almost to the swings now. My heart is

pounding. My chest is burning. But I can do this. I know I can! I sprint as hard as I can past the monkey bars, kicking up wood chips behind me.

"Meena is pulling ahead!" Dad shouts. He's right behind me! "She's going all out for the finish!"

I lunge for the swing set and slap it with a ping.

"It's Meena for the win!" Dad is yelling. He cups his hands over his mouth and makes crowd noises. "This is a total upset! An amazing result!"

I'm bent over, holding my side, panting and wincing and grinning all at once.

"Meena!" Dad holds out his fist like a microphone. "You were finished. You were done for! But somehow you beat out all the front-runners. How did you do it?" He holds his fist in front of my face.

For a few seconds I can't catch my breath. When I finally stand up straight, I still hear the imaginary crowd cheering. "I just kept running," I say into the mic. "No matter how hard it got, I just kept running as fast as I could."

I'm happy and worn out when Dad goes to pick up Rosie and go home. My whole body relaxes as I walk down the empty hall to class. I feel like a wrung-out washcloth. I give my head a shake and can still smell the fresh air in my hair.

Nobody except Mrs. D is in the third-grade room when I get there. "Hey, Meena," she says, looking up from her computer. "How'd it go today?"

"Fine. Is it lunchtime?"

"Yep. You can head on over."

Yes! I missed the whole morning—even handwriting! I pump my fist in the air.

"Come on back during recess," Mrs. D says. "You can start on your makeup work."

I groan and let my hand drop. "Can't we just call it good for today?"

She smirks at me. "It won't take you long. But tell you what. You can work on your valentine box instead if you want."

I snort. As if I'd let anyone see my box before it was ready.

I grab my lunch bag and head to the cafeteria. I wonder if Dad packed something fun, like those little pizzas you put together yourself, or if it's some kind of food you eat in an orderly fashion, like the cereal that looks like bales of hay. I just hope all the food groups are represented: red, orange, yellow, green, and bluish-purple. Mom says I have to get my colors from fruits and vegetables, but bluish-purple is hard to come by this time of year, because if I think they're paying five dollars for a pint of blueberries that have to get shipped all the way from South America, then I must be out of my mind. I've tried to get Mom to buy grape taffy instead, or that blueberry yogurt that comes in a tube, but sometimes there's no reasoning with her. If you ask me, this whole thing would be easier if she just let me bring jelly beans. They can even be in the same container. It's not like I have a thing about foods touching one another.

I'm very reasonable that way.

The noise from the lunchroom gets louder when I push through the door. Most of my class is crowded around a couple of tables. Eli sees me coming and scootches closer to Pedro to make room for me. His whole lunch tray is yellow: macaroni, corn, applesauce, and vanilla pudding. Lucky Dad packed for me! "Where were you?" Eli asks.

"At the hospital," I say, opening my bag. It turns out that talking about the MRI doesn't seem all that scary here. And anyway, nobody needs to know why I had one.

"Again? What for?"

"I had to go in this machine that takes pictures of your insides."

"You mean an X-ray?" Pedro asks.

"Kind of. But way bigger. And look." I push up the sleeve of my hoodie and hold out my arm so they can see the cotton ball Band-Aided to me.

Pedro's eyebrows shoot up. Next to him Lin stops and stares in the middle of trading her cookies for Maddy's chips.

"Whoa," Eli says, "you got a shot?"

"Uh-huh."

I hear the plunk of someone pulling the tab off a can and look down the table just in time to see the dark flicker of Sofía's lashes as she sets down her tiny can of apple juice. Was she looking at us?

She must have done Lunch Patrol without me again. My stomach tightens. I wonder what she does with her can tabs now that she doesn't save them for me.

"Why'd you need a shot?" Eli asks.

I take a Thermos out of my lunch bag. At the next table a second grader knocks over his milk. "I don't know," I say. "It makes your insides light up or something. Hey, Pedro, can I have that?"

He's twisting off the plastic wing-top thingy from his orange drink. I shoot Sofía a look when he hands it to me and stick it in my pocket. I don't need her stupid can tabs. I bet there's something cool I can do with this.

I open my Thermos. Spaghetti and meatballs! Dad sent baby carrots and green pepper slices and pineapple, too. I've almost got all the colors already, and then *bam!* I find a grape sucker at the bottom of my bag. I grab my plastic fork and dig in. The spaghetti flops all over. A few times I even drop it down the front of my shirt, but the sauce blends into the tie-dye, so I don't care.

I manage to get a little of every color by the time the bell rings, so I pack everything up and head out to play kickball with Eli and Pedro. No way am I missing recess to do my homework. But just as I'm pushing through the playground doors, I look back and see Sofía turn toward the classroom.

Of course she'll be there.

Then I wonder, what if she's not doing school-work at all? What if Sofía's using the extra time to work on her valentine box? If I can sneak a peek at it, I'll know exactly what I'm up against, and I can be absolutely certain mine turns out better than hers.

This is my chance to spy on her for a change!

I take my hands off the door and follow her down the hall.

"Valentine box or makeup work?" Mrs. D asks when I slip into my desk.

I glance at Sofía. She's getting out her markers, but I can't tell yet what she's working on. "I'll do my box at home," I say.

"Okay. Why don't you take out your language arts journal? This morning I asked everyone to write about something that made them smile today. You can work on that."

"Can I draw a picture with it?" I ask.

"Essay first."

"Can I use paint?" I ask.

She presses her lips together. "Let's see how far you get with your writing."

I guess she's not over the Green Splatter Incident yet.

She starts to walk away. "Mrs. D?" I call after her.

"It isn't a contest," she says over her shoulder, "and you don't get anything if yours is the best."

Darn it.

I sigh and take out my journal. I twirl my pencil around inside my little hand sharpener, watching the wood shavings spiral out. It's weird sitting in such an empty room—nothing but Sofía taking out some papers and Mrs. D leafing through worksheets. I bounce my knees under the desk and stare at the page, waiting for Inspiration.

But this isn't like *blank* paper. All those lines make me feel cramped and crowded. It's like they're just sitting there yelling *Do your work!* instead of *Make something beautiful!*

And Sofía isn't even working on her box as far as I can tell. All she's doing is drawing a boring rectangle. I watch her color it red. I should be out playing kickball.

But hang on. What if that's one of her valentines? I never even *thought* about making the best *valentines* in the class. How am I ever going to have time for that when I haven't even finished my box? And before I can do anything else, I have to get this dumb journal entry over with.

I pick up my pencil and tap it against my desk. Let's see. Something that made me smile today. Not the MRI, that's for sure, and definitely not the shot. Luckily for me, there was something.

You'll never guess what I did during school today. I didn't sit in class and practice handwriting like everybody else, that's for sure. I ran a race with my dad, and I totally won!

"Make sure you're using your best writing," Mrs. D says from her desk.

I look down at the page again. My writing never looks neat and curvy like it's supposed to. The letters are supposed to *flow* together, Mrs. D says. But mine always look like they're bumping into each other.

Stupid cursive. I don't get why the *b* looks like an *l* and why the *n* looks like an *m*—or how you're even supposed to tell the difference between the *g* and *q*.

Sofía peeks at a textbook on her desk and then starts drawing another rectangle—a pink one this time. Now I see. She's making a bar graph. I roll my eyes. What a waste of color. She clicks the lid back on the pink and snaps the marker into the tray. She likes to keep them nestled in their original package and take them out one at a time. Sofía looks at the book, reaches for her purple marker, and draws another rectangle next to the others. She clicks the lid back on.

Mrs. D stands up from her desk. "I need to go make a few photocopies," she says. "Are you two okay on your own?"

Sofía and I glance at each other, then look away. After Mrs. D leaves the room, we sit there. I keep thumping my pencil on my notebook: *Tap-tap, tap-tap*. Sofía keeps opening and closing different colored markers: *Click-snap, click-snap*.

I can't think of anything else to write in my

journal. And I don't want to use pencil. Sofía's paper is getting more colorful by the second, even though she's just doing math. The rectangles on her bar graph look like colorful skyscrapers.

I can't stand it anymore.

I take out my markers. I'll make my picture first. *That* will give me an Inspiration. And maybe when Mrs. D sees it, she won't make me write out what it was like to run this morning, because she'll just be able to tell. Maybe my picture will be so beautiful that she'll even clip me up for a change!

I dump all my markers out on my desk. I want them where I can see them, and where they can see me. I can't use all of them at once, but I want them to know I'll get around to all of them eventually.

I turn the page of my journal and get started. I draw my dad running across the playground. I'm just barely in front of him, reaching for the swings, my hair flying behind me in rainbow streaks. Even though it was cloudy out, I make the sky bright blue with the sun shining above us. I breathe in the smell of the markers and listen to the click of the caps. The more clicks I make, the more colorful my picture gets.

I'm so busy drawing that I don't know how long Sofía has been watching me when I catch her. "What?" I say.

She looks down.

I straighten up. "Did Mrs. D tell you to spy on me?"

Her eyes flick back up. "No!" She bends over her desk again. "It's nothing."

"Then why were you staring?"

She takes the lid off her blue marker and hunches over even further. "I was just making sure you're still there," she says in a small voice.

I roll my eyes. "I'm sitting right in front of you."

"Yeah, but . . ." She looks at me with a crinkle in her forehead. "Sometimes you space out."

"So? Everybody does that."

She shakes her head. "It's not the same. It's like you're not even there. Sometimes you make this weird hissing noise, too. Or you drool a little."

I feel my face getting hot. "You're making that up," I say.

She shakes her head. "It happened with your President Portrait."

"What did?"

"You went . . . blank inside. Your hands got twitchy, and your eyes blinked a lot. And when Mrs. D asked for your paper, you just kept scribbling."

I glare at her. First she abandons me, and now she makes up lies? She's just being mean for no reason! If any of that were true, I'd remember it. Or someone would have told me, right?

But I don't remember riding to the hospital

in an ambulance. And Eli said I ignored Mrs. D when she asked for my portrait. Why didn't I hear her? Why did I scribble purple all over my picture? And why did I get clipped down for not following directions?

What's the matter with me?

I think of the white smudge on the X-ray skull. I try to push the image away and concentrate on my work again, but all of a sudden the space between my journal and my body seems to stretch out, like a tunnel that's closing in. My legs are jumpy and

want to run away, but I'm stuck here, at this desk, just like I was stuck in the cramped tube of the MRI machine. But this time the banging and the whirring are in my head, and it doesn't matter who else is in the room, because this is only happening to me.

I'm starting to gasp for air. I put my hands over my face and press hard, forcing myself to take a deep breath, then another. When my heart stops feeling like it will pound right out of my chest, I open my eyes again.

I look down at my picture: me running across the playground with Dad.

Then I take out my purple crayon and start rubbing it over the entire page.

Stupid spot in my head. Stupid *something* that ruins everything.

I grit my teeth and rub purple over the blades of grass and my perfect shade of sky. I rub it over my rainbow hair until the colors are all drowning in purple.

That's when I hear Sofía whisper, "Is that why you were gone this morning? Because you space out sometimes?"

My stomach starts to bubble. "None of your business."

She clicks the lid on her red marker and just holds it, looking at me. "Is that why they took pictures of your insides?"

"It's not because of that." I snap the words out, because I am *not* going to cry. "It's because I had a *seizure*. I had to ride in an ambulance, and I woke up in the hospital, and now everybody watches me all the time in case there are *fireworks in my brain!*"

"Meena."

I look up. Mrs. D is standing next to me, holding a stack of papers. She squats down beside my desk and puts a hand on my arm. "What are you supposed to be doing?" she asks, her voice so soft I can barely hear her.

I feel the corners of my mouth pulling down. "My journal," I mutter.

"And how's it coming so far?"

I take a quick peek over at the clip chart. I'm at Ready for Anything now, but Go to the Principal is just waiting for me at the bottom. I didn't write my essay. And I ruined my picture. Again. On purpose this time. I close my notebook before Mrs. D can see it.

She nods and stands up. "I think maybe you two should head outside for the last few minutes of recess," Mrs. D says. "Go get some fresh air."

I don't wait for her to change her mind. I jump up from my desk and head into the hall.

"Just stay together until you're outside," Mrs. D calls after me.

I am *not* waiting for Sofía. I grab my jacket

from my cubby and keep walking.

"Is that why you need help with the lunch count?" Sofía asks from behind me. Like she cares.

"I don't need help," I tell her over my shoulder. I fast-walk down the hall so I won't say the rest of my thoughts out loud.

Especially from you.

15

The rest of my day has way more Downs than Ups.

We don't get to do relay races in gym because we have to watch a dumb video on nutrition. Mrs. D makes me take my language arts journal home to finish it. And to top it off, when Mom and Rosie meet me at the front doors after school, Rosie shrieks and runs to Sofía! Like she's *her* sister instead of mine!

Sofía makes an *oof* sound when Rosie slams into her. "Hey, Rosie Posey," she says.

"Where have you been?" demands Rosie. She jumps up and down. "Are you coming over?"

Sofía shoots me a worried look.

She shouldn't worry. I'm not inviting her. I cross my arms, feeling the hot lava start to bubble in my stomach again.

She shakes her head at Rosie. "Not today."

"Aw," Rosie groans. Then she lifts up her arms to Sofía and starts to dance around. "Twirl me!" she says.

Sofía grins and takes her by the hands. She starts whirling Rosie around like she used to, faster and faster until they're twirling so hard that Rosie's feet lift off the ground. She squeals. Sofía swings her around a few more times until Rosie's feet start to scrape against the sidewalk, and she stumbles and lands on her bottom, laughing.

"You okay, squirt?" Sofía says, offering her a hand.

Hey, that's *my* nickname for her! I step in between them. "You don't get to call her that," I say. I pull Rosie up and start dragging her away.

"Meena," Mom gasps as we pass her. "What's gotten into you?"

Rosie turns and waves over her shoulder. "Bye, Sofía!"

Traitor. I shake her hand loose, my stomach boiling all the way to the end of the block.

It's not until I turn the corner toward home that I finally get an Up.

It's recycling day! Big green bins are lined up on the curb. I run to the first one and look inside. It's mostly broken-down cardboard boxes. The next one is empty cans and water bottles. I'm not even sure what I'm looking for until I see an egg carton sitting right on top of the next bin. I reach in and grab it. There's only a little bit of shell inside and hardly any dried-up yolk gunk. I open and close it a few times, feeling the itchy start of an Inspiration tingling in my fingertips.

"Put it back," Mom says, coming up behind me.

"I need it for my valentine box."

"You're not dragging that home, Meena. It's trash."

"Yeah, but it's not *litter*," I say. I'm about to explain the difference, but she gives me her I'm-not-messing-around-here look, and points back at the bin. I let out a huffy breath and drop the carton.

Rosie runs ahead of us while I drag my feet past the rest of the bins. I guess Mom wants to change the subject, because she bumps her shoulder against mine and switches to a concerned voice. "Something going on with Sofía?" she asks.

I make one of those wavy shrugs that doesn't mean anything.

"Okay. . . ." She's quiet. "Then, do you want to talk about this morning?"

I stick my hands in my pockets. I do *not* want to talk about it. The MRI was the biggest Down of my day.

"I guess we didn't give you much idea what to expect," Mom says. "I'm sorry. I think that made it even scarier."

I doubt it. Even if I knew the shot was coming, I probably would have worried about it the whole time I was in the tube. "Why couldn't they use the pictures they already had?" I ask.

"Those don't show as much detail as the ones they took today," she says. "It's pretty amazing how much they can see with an MRI. Did you know that Dad had one when he hurt his knee?"

I look up at her. "When?"

"A few years ago. Remember how he wore a brace for a while? And Aunt Kathy had one just last year."

"She had an MRI?" I ask. "What for?"

"Her back was hurting her, and they couldn't figure out why. They wanted to make sure she didn't have a tumor on her spine."

"What's a tumor?"

Mom's feet do a little stutter, like she tripped over something, but when I look back at the sidewalk, there's nothing there.

She doesn't answer. "What's a tumor?" I ask again.

Mom hesitates. When she finally responds, she sounds careful—like she's stepping over broken glass. "It's something growing inside your body that isn't supposed to be there," she says.

There's that word again: *something*. That's what they called the white smudge on the X-ray picture of my skull. I think about a *something* in Aunt Kathy's back. I imagine it white and smeary, snaking up her spine, tangling around it. Just thinking of it makes me feel like there's a clump of weeds in my stomach. "What was wrong with her back?" I ask.

"There was just some swelling in her vertebrae."

"So she didn't have a tumor?"

"No."

"Do I?"

Mom blinks a bunch of times, but she doesn't look down at me. And she doesn't say anything else.

The worry weeds in my stomach grow into vines. They climb up through my chest and into my throat. I try to swallow them down. "Is that what they were looking for this morning?" I ask.

When she finally answers, she says each word very slowly. "They were looking for anything that shouldn't be there."

I turn and stare straight ahead. I keep walking, step by step, but I can feel the worry weeds spreading up my neck, all the way to the top of my head. They stop right at the place where my doctor rested her hand. *This is the spot*, she said. *Right about here.* I imagine that the spot starts to pulse, like it's sending out an SOS.

Mom tries to put her arm around me, but I stumble ahead of her. I don't even wonder what's in the rest of the green bins.

When we get home, Rosie grabs Pink Pony off

the kitchen counter and runs to the living room to play. Mom goes straight to her computer, but I stand by the back door in a daze. My heart is pounding, and I can't think of what I'm supposed to be doing. Finally, I remember to hang my backpack on its hook. I take off my jacket and put it in the closet. I toe off one shoe, then the other, and put them on the rack one by one. I stare at all my nice and neat, put-away things.

It has a name. The *something* in my head. The Thing That Shouldn't Be There.

Tumor.

Is it a tumor? What if it is? Maybe that's not so bad. Last summer I got a sliver in my finger from a splintery picnic table at the park. It was a Thing That Shouldn't Be There too, but it wasn't such a big deal. Mom took it out with tweezers.

Although it seemed like she was pinching and digging around the tip of my finger forever while I whimpered and squirmed and Dad tried to crack jokes.

I hold out my hands and stare. I can't remember which finger it was. The tweezers didn't even leave a mark.

What do they use to take out a tumor? Will *it* leave a mark?

Mom calls to me from the kitchen table. "Come get started on your homework, hon."

The worry weeds branch out from my chest into my arms. I feel like I'm sleepwalking when I unzip my backpack, take out my homework, and head to the table. Raymond is there next to my craft supplies. He seems droopy, like it hurts his feelings that I don't take him to school. He's not even looking at me.

Mom sits down at her computer. "Spelling?" she asks. "Math?"

My chest gets tight. "Can I do it later?" I ask.

"You know the rules." She puts on her glasses. "Come on. I'll stay with you."

My hand floats up to the top of my head.

It isn't like a splinter, I realize—the *something* in my head. It didn't come from the outside. And I can't feel it. Nobody can even see it.

So what will they use to get it out?

I swallow. It won't be tweezers.

My arms break out in goose bumps. "I don't want to do this right now," I say, dropping my folder on the table and taking a step back. My voice is just a squeak.

Mom glances up from her computer. "You'll feel better once you get started."

I think of those pointy instruments they use at the dentist's office. I think of the big rusty saw hanging in our garage.

All of a sudden my ears fill with static, and

everything starts closing in, like I'm looking through binoculars. I shut my eyes and put my hands over my ears. "I don't want to do this!" I yell.

"Meena—" Mom says.

"Don't make me do this!" My mind is swirling with pictures now—scissors and axes and drills.

"Honey—"

I keep yelling. "Don't make me do this! Please, please, I don't want to do this!"

I hear Mom's chair scraping away from the table. I want to run, but her arms wrap around me, and I'm trapped. She squeezes so tight that I couldn't take my hands off my ears even if I wanted to.

Which I don't.

I can't get away. I strain against her arms, trying to break free. Tears are burning my throat.

"I just—" I'm panting into her chest now. "I want to work on my valentine box," I say. "Can't I just work on my box?"

I'm stiff and shivery, gulping in air.

Mom holds me. She might even be holding me up. But she loosens her arms enough to start rocking back and forth with me. She starts taking big breaths, really big, deep, in-and-out breaths. I feel her chest moving up and down, and after a while I start to breathe like that too. *In and out. In and out.* For a long time we just stand there breathing and rocking. My heart starts to slow down. My body starts to slump. Mom keeps rocking.

I don't know how long it is before I remember to hold myself up. I crack my eyes open a little. I take my hands off my ears.

Mom looks down at me with tears in her eyes. She tucks a strand of purple hair behind my ear. "What do you need from me, honey?" she asks.

I take a shuddery breath. "I need an egg carton," I say.

She blinks, then rubs my arms up and down before she goes to the refrigerator. She empties the eggs into a bowl and comes back and hands me the carton.

"And I need you to go play with Rosie," I say.

"I don't mind staying here with you."

I shake my head. "I want to be alone. I'll stay in the kitchen, but alone. Okay?"

It seems like a long time before Mom nods, very slowly. "Okay."

She heads into the living room, and I'm all by myself. Finally. I pull a chair to the table and set the carton in front of me. I don't even know why I need this thing. I'm not feeling sparkly or creative. I'm slumpy and tired and colorless.

But without anybody watching me, it seems like there's more air in the room, and my skin feels relaxed again instead of prickly and spied on. So

I just keep breathing and waiting. Once or twice I look at Raymond to see if he has any bright ideas.

And after a while I need some paint.

I use white—which is weird for me. It soaks into the gray cardboard fast, making it clean and bright. I even paint the inside. But it's still only halfway dry when I start globbing You-Must-Be-Crazy Glue on the front of each egg-bump. I open up my jar of can tabs. I stick one in each blob of glue, then run to the bathroom for some of those tiny hair bands. I pick out all different colors and glue them right on top of the tabs.

I don't know how long I work, but this time I know I don't space out. I remember the smell of the paint and the feel of the glue turning hard on my fingertips. I remember the bright swirl of wrappers on my box and the crinkle they made when I smoothed them out. I even remember singing about the wheels on the bus going round and round. If Mom is peeking at me sometimes, I don't notice her until my box is almost finished. By then, it's dark out. The windows are black and steaming up. Mom is at the stove, dumping broccoli into a pot.

"Is it dinnertime?" I ask.

"Almost," Mom says. "How's your box coming along?"

I sit back. "Wanna see?"

She gives the pot a stir and comes over and

laughs. "It's not a box. It's a *beast*." She leans in closer. "Oh my goodness. Are those teeth?" She makes a little gasp. "Are those *braces*?"

I grin. "With rainbow rubber bands."

Mom shakes her head and smiles.

"There's more," I say. "Can you bring me a valentine?"

She picks up a piece of mail from the counter. "How about a water bill? Will that do?" She holds it out.

I shake my head. "You do it."

"Do what?"

"Feed him."

Mom looks at the box again. Then she lifts open the egg carton teeth and sticks the envelope in through the slot I cut. There's a little thump when it lands at the bottom of the box. The lid drops closed like a chomp.

Mom laughs. "It eats valentines," she says. "That's awesome." She ruffles my rainbow hair. "You're really something, you know that?"

I smile at my box. He looks like he's smiling back at me.

I bet he's good enough to win.

16

I dream about my valentine box that night. And as soon as I wake up the next morning, I realize he isn't ready to take to school. If he's going to eat valentines, I need to cut a trapdoor to get them back out. Plus, I need to make him some wings, because it turns out that guy can fly!

My arms don't jerk even once while I'm getting ready for school, which is an Up. Dad makes pancakes for breakfast too. That's another. Plus he adds leftover fruit salad to the batter, so I get the whole rainbow at once!

I'm feeling good and colorful by the time I get to school. Right away I spot someone's box on the ground by the basketball hoop, even though our party isn't until tomorrow. It's just a shoebox slopped with red paint, which makes me laugh. I'd know that box was Pedro's even if you lined up a mile of valentine boxes. He's as lazy about decorating as I am about handwriting. I spot him playing horse with Maddy and wave until he sees me. "It's graded on effort," I yell at him, pointing at his box. "You didn't put in any effort!"

"Yes, I did," he hollers back, dribbling the ball while he pivots away from Maddy. "Look inside!"

I open the lid. Instead of leaving it plain, he slopped paint in there, too. Not bad, considering this is Pedro we're talking about. I grin and give him a thumbs-up. He gives me one back and makes a break for the basket.

Eli gets to the playground next. At first I think he's carrying a bundle of firewood, but when he gets closer, I can see it's his box! He glued sticks all over the sides and made it look like a log cabin.

"You like it?" he asks, holding it out to me.

I run my hand over it, feeling the bumps of bark. "You're the only kid I know who would cover your box in nature," I say. I lift the lid. The inside is lined with pine needles. "Are those from your yard?" I ask.

"Yep."

"Nice," I say. I stick my nose in and take a deep, Christmassy breath. "And very fragrant."

"Plus, after Valentine's Day, I can make it into a habitat."

"For what?"

He shrugs. "Whatever I find next."

Not everybody has their box ready today, but enough kids show up with theirs that I start to notice a trend. It seems like every box matches the person who made it. Lin's is wrapped in tinfoil and looks like a rocket, because she loves anything to do with outer space. Aiden made one that's covered in real candy hearts and gumdrops, because all that kid eats is sugar. I wonder if my valentine box matches me.

I wonder if Sofía's will match her.

I try not to look like I'm waiting for Sofía. When I see her walking with her mom way down the sidewalk, I get very busy looking through the wood chips with Eli, chewing on the strings of my hoodie. By the time I turn and sneak a peek through my rainbow hair, I see something pink bobbing toward the playground. The sun glares into my eyes, and I can't get a good look. Then the bell rings, and I lose her in a crowd of kids pushing into the building.

I follow everyone inside. While I'm shoving my coat into my cubby, I catch a glimpse of pink and the back of Sofía's head disappearing into the classroom. She's setting her box on the project table when I get in there. She steps back, and all I can see at first is a whole bunch of pink feathers. Then I finally get a good look, and my heart starts to beat harder.

It's a flamingo. She made her box into a flamingo.

It's got a long, curvy neck that must be some kind of hose covered in pink fluff, although I don't know why it doesn't just flop over. The whole feather-box looks like it's hovering over the table, because it's balanced on these skinny legs that seem to be—

My stomach squeezes.

Coat hangers.

Seriously? When am I going to start using those things? They're a miracle product!

The rest of the class is starting to crowd around Sofía's box. I can't help it. I move closer, too. That flamingo pulls me over like a magnet.

"If you don't have a job to do," Mrs. D says, "please take your seats."

One by one everyone else moves away from the table. Before I go, I quick lift up the lid of Sofía's box to see if there's anything inside.

Of course there is.

She lined it with tissue paper and glitter. There's even a velvety pink pillow at the bottom for the valentines, like the kind a princess dog would sit on.

I go to my desk. Lin collects all our worksheets. Aiden sharpens the pencils. But I can't stop staring at that flamingo. Deep down in the pit of my stomach, the lava starts to bubble.

My box has to be better than that.

He *has* to be.

Mrs. D fills out the lunch slip and hands it to

me. I head right into the hall without even waiting for Sofía. I go straight to fifth grade, take the slip off their door, and turn around.

She's right behind me. Her poufy flower headband is pink today.

I guess she matches her box too. They're both tall and pink and perfect.

My stomach is almost boiling up into my throat now. I want to yell. I want to kick something! But instead I smile at Sofía with just my mouth, very calm. I bet if she looked closely, she'd see steam leaking out through my teeth.

"I like your flamingo," I say. My voice is shiny and soft like melted butter.

She doesn't say anything at first. She just looks at me with a crinkly forehead. Then her forehead smoothes out, and she smiles. "Thanks," she says. I can see the rainbow rubber bands on her braces.

I walk to the fourth-grade room. I get their slip, come back to the hallway, and scowl at her. "My box eats flamingos," I say.

I move down the hall. I pass the third-grade room, knock at second, and get their slip. But when I try to head to first grade, Sofía is standing there with her arms crossed.

"Why are you so mean to me?" she says.

I try to go around her.

She blocks my way. "I never asked to do Lunch

Patrol, you know," she says. "I'm only doing it because Mrs. D told me to."

"Whatever," I say. I know she'd never do anything with me that she didn't have to. Not anymore.

"It's true!" she says. "It's not my fault you need help."

"I don't need help," I say, gritting my teeth.

Sofía's next words shoot toward me like arrows. She points her chin out. "What's the matter with you anyway?"

"Nothing's the matter with me," I snap. I push past her and storm into first grade without knocking.

I'm getting that underwater feeling again. My throat is starting to close, and I can't get enough air. My hand is shaking when I get the lunch slip, and by the time I get back to the hallway, my ears are roaring with static.

This is the spot, I imagine a voice saying. *Right about here.*

I clamp my hands onto the top of my head. I don't want to think about it.

But it's like a shadow lurking in the corner, no matter what I'm doing. It's not solid and bright and real. It's blurry like the X-ray picture. It's foggy and see-through like the Magic Mist. But I always feel it there, even when I close my eyes.

Especially then.

I start heading back down the hall, but my chest is tight and I'm gasping for air like I've been sprinting. I only get halfway to the office before I have to stop and catch my breath.

Our President Portraits are hanging there in the hall. I see President Meena holding the cake with rainbow sprinkles, colorful streaks in her hair, purple scribbles all over her face.

I cover my eyes and lean against the wall.

What *is* the matter with me?

I wish I could ask Sofía. I wish I could ask why my arms jerk and why I scribble when I don't mean to. I wish I could ask why she'd rather be perfect than be my friend. What's the matter with *me*?

I'd give anything to talk to the Sofía who drew and played and raced with me—the one I'd been friends with since kindergarten.

But I don't know her anymore.

I open my eyes. This Sofía is standing with her hands on her hips, her lips pressed tightly together. "What did I ever do to you?" she asks.

I can barely get enough air to answer. I should say, *You stopped being my friend*, but I don't want to care, and I don't want to cry.

So instead I clench my jaw and say, "You beat me. You beat me at everything."

She shakes her head. "I'm not trying to beat you."

I know she isn't. She doesn't even have to try. And the truth is, it doesn't matter if she has better handwriting or crazier hair or more colorful teeth than me. It doesn't matter that her clip is always higher than mine.

I just want her to be my friend.

But that's not what I say.

"You're supposed to have Ups and Downs," I say, gripping the little papers. "We're *all* supposed to. But you never have anything but Ups!"

Her face freezes. "You don't know what I have," she whispers.

"I know you never clip down," I say. "You never get in trouble, and you never get any tumors in your brain—but there might be one in mine!"

At first her face stays frozen. Then she blinks, and it starts to melt into something like surprise. "Meena—" she says. She takes a teeny step toward me.

I jump back and the volcano inside me explodes. I feel hot lava flying around in my stomach and flooding my chest. I feel it shining out my eyes and streaming out the ends of my hair.

Why shouldn't Sofía have a Down for a change? I wish I could snap her pin off the clip chart or rip the feathers right off her flamingo. I want to do something that hurts her as much as she hurt me.

But I can only think of one thing.

"I'm not making you a valentine," I say.

She takes a step back, her eyes wide.

"I'll make one for everyone else, but I'm not making one for you."

"You have to," she says. "It's the rule."

"I don't care. Mrs. D can clip me all the way down to Principal, and I still won't make you one. And you know what else?" I lean right up to her. "My box will be the best one in the class. Even better than yours."

"It isn't a contest," she whispers.

"Of *course* it's a contest," I yell, and stomp off down the hall.

17

The hurt keeps boiling inside me. All morning I wriggle in my seat, feeling the steam pouring out of my skin.

The lava churns during spelling. Our words are full of letters that Shouldn't Be There—words like *wrong* and *doubt*. I write and erase and write and erase so many times that my paper turns crumbly and gray.

The heat is still there at recess. I don't look for beautiful trash or play kickball or race. I jump rope by myself—up and down and up and down until I'm sweaty and panting. Even that doesn't snuff it out.

Then, in the afternoon, when Mrs. D starts our read-aloud book, I slump over my desk and feel my whole body throbbing, just like when I bang my elbow and that first zing of pain turns into a heartbeat instead.

I try to think about my valentine box. I imagine how our igloo will look when it's finished. I try to remember exactly how many stripes Raymond has in his fur. But I can't get my mind to focus on anything. It's like the worry is under my skin or ringing in my ears, and nothing I can think of is noisy enough to cover it up.

It reminds me of how music couldn't cover up the banging sounds in the MRI.

All afternoon I can feel Sofía sitting across from me at her desk. Even though I don't look at her. Not once, all day.

After school I walk home way ahead of Mom and Rosie, like I'm Line Leader of my family.

I get right to work on my box. I cut the trapdoor. I make wings with waxed paper. Then I take off the lid and look inside.

I think about the paint in Pedro's box and the pine needles in Eli's and the velvety pillow in Sofía's. I stare at the not-colorful, not-fragrant, not-pretty inside of my empty box for a long time, waiting for Inspiration.

Only this time, the idea that finally comes to me doesn't feel like the sun rising in my chest, or like bells ringing in my arms and legs.

It feels like the hot lava that bubbled in my stomach all day cooling off and turning to rock.

I take Raymond up to my workshop, dig around until I find what I need, and then leave him there so he can't see what I do next.

I head back to the kitchen dragging that old feather scarf I found in the trash. It's stringy and crunchy and still smells like tuna. But I just start plucking.

I grab fistfuls of pink and sprinkle them inside. I squeeze You-Must-Be-Crazy Glue in there and throw in more feathers. I pluck and squeeze and sprinkle until my box is so full, there isn't even room for valentines. Then I glue a few more feathers sticking out of the egg carton. I put the lid on, sit back, and take a look.

My box is grinning a mean grin. He's full of feathers now. He even has pink bits of feathers stuck in his teeth.

He looks like he just ate a flamingo.

I work on my valentines the rest of the afternoon. I don't feel lovey or friendly, but I cut as neatly as I can anyway. I add loads of ribbon and glitter and tape a piece of chocolate to each one. I even spend extra time using my very best writing, which takes forever.

Sofía will be sorry she isn't getting one of these.

Mom shines the counter while I work. She checks her phone. She stands by the refrigerator eating stalks of celery, one after another. They disappear into her mouth like pencils getting ground up in a sharpener. For a while she and Rosie play concentration at the other end of the table, but Rosie wins so many times that she gets bored and wanders off. Mom picks up the cards and shuffles and reshuffles them until her phone starts to ring. "Hello?" she shouts, grabbing for it. "Hello, I'm here!"

Her face gets droopy.

"Oh, hi." She rubs her hand across her head. "No, not yet. I even tried calling her office." Mom sags against the counter. "Just get something for the kids. I'm not hungry."

Dad's carrying a pizza box when he gets home a little while later. He raises his eyebrows at Mom. She shakes her head, her mouth a straight line. "Maybe she'll call after hours," he says.

"Or maybe she'll make us wait another day."

Dad sets down the pizza and rubs Mom's shoulders. She lets out a breath. Then they both turn and look at me.

I stop clipping right at the point of a paper heart.

They both have the same look on their face. They look just like Eli's guinea pig when you lift him out of his cage, before he remembers that you've always been nice to him and there's nothing to worry about.

They look like a guinea pig when he's scared.

The lava rock in my stomach turns to a sheet of ice.

Nobody eats much at dinner. My stomach is too full of rocks. Mom's must be full of celery, and Rosie stopped liking cheese again this week. But even Dad doesn't eat more than a couple of bites. He just sits there flipping my purple marker over and across his fingers.

Then the phone rings.

Mom jumps. Dad lets go of the marker.

And I don't know why, but I lunge across the table and grab the phone.

"Hello?" I say.

There's a pause. "Well, hello," someone says. "Is this Meena? This is Dr. Suri."

I drop the phone.

I knew the voice even before she said her name.

I've heard it a hundred times. I hear it at night when I'm lying awake. I heard it today in the hall. *This is the spot. Right about here.*

I don't want to know why my doctor is calling.

"Hello?" Mom says, scooping up the phone. "Hello? Yes, I'm here!"

I climb down from the table. I take a wobbly step backward, grab my valentine box, and run for the stairs.

I slam the door of my workshop.

There must be something else I can do to this box.

He's so pretty on the outside. The way the light hits the candy wrappers, they look like the oil splotch in the driveway—like every color at once. But what about when you look inside?

I open him up and see all those mean feathers, and my throat tightens. All the boxes at school today matched the people who made them.

Does my box match me? What's inside of me?

Mean feathers? Angry lava? A tumor?

Who cares if you're covered in rainbows when you're full of Things That Shouldn't Be There?

I have to fix this. I drop to my knees and start yanking out the feathers. Raymond is sitting on the floor, staring back at me. My eyes fill with tears, but I can still see the pink fluff that floats in the air and feel the prickly bits stuck to the bottom.

I start scratching them out. The pointy parts get stuck under my nails, but I just keep at it. I wish I could scratch all the bad stuff out of everything — all the feathers and the lava and the tumors. I wish I could fix my body. My bracelet. Whatever broke between Sofía and me.

But I can't. All I can do is pull every last feather out of this box.

There might be a tumor inside me, but my box won't be full of another single thing that's mean or ugly. And neither will I.

I sit back on my heels and remember Sofía's flamingo box. I think about the million, billion Ups she's had since she stopped being my friend. I imagine her clip, sitting at the top of the chart, and jealous lava starts to bubble again.

But the truth is, I don't want Sofía's Ups.

I want my own.

I close my eyes and remember racing with Dad. I think about breathing with Mom and cuddling with Rosie. I imagine looking through the wood chips with Eli.

I want the Ups I already have, I realize — the ones I've barely noticed since this whole thing started.

I wipe my eyes on the back of my arm and look inside my box. It's not perfect in there. It never will be.

But I can make it beautiful. I can fill my box with the most wonderful things in the world. Because that's what I do. That's what I'm good at.

I make beautiful things from trash. I take beat-up, worn-out, used-up things, and I give them a second chance. I make them better and more colorful than they were before.

That's when I'm At My Best.

I start grabbing bottle caps and Easter grass and lids from dried-up markers. I start shoving in wads of tinfoil and bits of blue glass with the edges worn down and a ball of the red wax you take off cheese. I dump in all the beads I pulled out of the mud and the plastic wing Pedro twisted off his drink bottle.

I need them all.

I want to stay here forever with my trash. I'd fill up on every color in the world and be ready for whatever comes next. I wish I could just work on my box, and that this time would go on and on—before I find out about the *something* in my brain. And before any other scary thing can happen, I get up, go to my window, and breathe on it until my own Magic Mist appears. Then I swipe my finger across the glass to make an arc, and then another, and another.

I stare at my see-through rainbow and hold the word *please* in my heart.

The fog disappears, the picture dries into

colorless streaks, and Dad is shouting up the stairs at me.

"Meena Zee!" he says. "Come down here."

Mom and Dad are waiting for me.

"We have some news," Mom says when I'm halfway down the stairs.

They're holding out their arms to me. But I can't tell if this is going to be a good-news hug or a we're-so-sorry hug, so I squeeze Raymond instead and walk right past them. Rosie is on the floor of the living room with Pink Pony, coloring.

"Not yet," I say, my heart beating faster. "It's story time." I flop down onto the couch. "Come on. Someone has to tell a story."

Rosie does a little cheer and hops up from the floor. Mom and Dad look at each other then back at me. "Are you sure that's what you want?" Dad asks.

I cross my arms. "That's what I want," I say, trying to keep my voice steady.

He nods. "Okay, deal."

They come over and sit on either side of me. Rosie squishes in too. We're one big pile of family now, everyone sitting on everyone else.

Whatever is going to happen next, I want it to happen here.

"Rosie, why don't you get us started?" Dad asks.

Rosie smiles and nuzzles against Mom's shoulder. "Once upon a time," she says.

Dad looks right at me.

I shut my eyes. My body starts to shake, but I take a deep breath, nestle down, and wait. I want to hear the story. Nothing else. Just this. Only this.

He clears his throat. "Once upon a time," he says, "there was a little girl who made big messes."

Someone ruffles my hair.

"She made such big messes," Dad says, "that her parents had to make weird rules, like 'no bringing home trash from the neighbors.' And 'no coloring people's hair with marker.'"

"That's just like Meena!" Rosie says.

"Is it?" Dad asks.

"But she's not little. She's a big girl."

"That's true," Dad says. "She is a big girl."

Someone gives me a squeeze. It might be every-one.

The shaking moves up into my throat. My teeth start to chatter.

"One day," Dad says, "some doctors had to look to see if there were any messes inside that big girl. They used special machines to see inside. Fancy machines. Machines that made her very scared. And what do you think they saw?"

"What?" says Rosie.

Lava, I think. *Ripped feathers. A tumor.*

"Did they see the penny she swallowed when she was a baby?" asks Dad.

"No," Rosie says.

"Did they see the peas she stuck up her nose when she was a toddler?" Dad asks.

"No," giggles Rosie.

"Did they see a shadowy spot inside her head?" Dad asks.

Rosie is quiet. Then in a tiny voice she asks, "Did they?"

"Yes, they did."

I blink and look at Rosie. She's looking back at me with crinkly eyebrows. I swallow.

Then I take her hand and rest it on top of my head. I put my hand on top of hers. "This is the spot," I say. "Right about here."

Rosie eyes go wide.

Mom rests her hand on top of mine. Dad puts his hand on top of Mom's.

Nobody says anything. It's like they're all making a silent wish on me.

I make one too.

Then one by one we all take our hands away.

"But as for that shadowy spot in the girl's head," Dad says. He waits until we all look at him again. "It turned out to be nothing at all."

For a few seconds I'm so scared of what he's saying that my mind tries to shoo the words away like pigeons, until they slip through and land anyway, and I hear them.

Nothing at all.

I blink. "Really?"

Rosie starts to bounce. Dad is smiling a watery-eyed smile. "Really," he says.

"The thing in my head . . . ," I say it very slowly, wanting to be sure. "It isn't anything?"

"It's a bump," Mom says, wiping her eyes. She's smiling too. "Lots of people have one. It's just the normal shape of your skull. It's nothing to worry about."

I stare at them. Rosie jumps off the couch and

skips around the coffee table, dragging Pink Pony by the mane. The rock in my stomach cracks down the middle. Little bits of it loosen and break away.

I should be jumping for joy or skipping like Rosie. I should feel like I do on my birthday, when I've waited and waited and then I wake up and it's finally *here*.

But I don't.

"Then why did I have a seizure?" I ask. "Why do my arms jerk in the morning, and why did Sofía say I space out sometimes like I'm not even there?"

"She said that?" Mom asks.

I nod.

She and Dad look at each other. Then Mom sighs and brushes the hair away from my forehead. "We don't know, honey," she says. "But I'll tell you what the doctor thinks." She takes hold of my hands. "She thinks you have epilepsy."

My stomach starts to tighten again. "Is that a thing in my head?"

"No," Mom says firmly. "It's not like a tumor."

"It's more like the *kind* of brain you have," Dad says. "It just works differently from other people's." He grins. "But we knew that already, right?"

"Does that mean I'll have more seizures?" I ask.

Rosie stops skipping and listens.

"Maybe," Mom says, looking at both of us. "Dr. Suri wants us to do another test to see if that's likely.

But if you do, we can manage it. You might end up needing to take medicine to prevent seizures. And you'll just have to be careful about certain activities."

"Like what?"

"Like swimming."

"And piloting jet planes," Dad says. "No more of that."

"Meena flies planes?" Rosie says. "No fair!"

"What about doing Lunch Patrol by myself?" I ask. "And going to bed later than Rosie? And making stuff in my workshop?"

"You can do all that," Mom says. "Even if you have seizures."

I squint at her. "What about everybody spying on me?"

Mom looks sideways at Dad. "Actually," she says, "the doctor thinks we went a little overboard with that."

My mouth spreads into a big grin. Because if I don't have people following me around all the time, I have a *zillion* things to do!

I have treasures to find, and recycling bins to look through. And let's face it—my rainbow hair could use a touch-up.

All that will have to wait, though, because right now I'm starting to feel like a slump. I sink farther into the couch. I'm so tired that if they sent me to bed early one more time, I wouldn't even mind.

I still want that story, though. I want to hug Raymond as hard as I can and cuddle up with my family. And if Rosie doesn't stick her elbow in my face, she can sit right next to me and listen to the one where Eeyore gets a present. It's nothing but a popped balloon and an empty honey jar—trash that no one else wanted—but it's the best gift he ever got.

And after that, when Rosie goes to bed, and I get to stay up later, because I'm nine, and nobody needs to spy on me after all, I have to do one more thing.

I have to make another valentine.

My box is ready.

I carry him to school all by myself. Dad and Rosie don't wait for me, and I'm so far behind them that I'm almost late. Also, it turns out when you jump for joy in a box of packing peanuts that somebody left on the curb, they break into teeny bits that stick to your body like *magnets*, no matter how long you stand there trying to brush them off!

I'm still half a block from school when I hear the first bell ring. Styrofoam dust flies off me while I run the rest of the way. Treasures rattle inside my box. I have just enough time to bust through the front doors, fast-walk to my class, and set my box down on the project table before the late bell rings.

Eli raises his eyebrows at me. Lin is already picking up worksheets. Aiden is at the sharpener. Mrs. D is counting hands for school lunch—only seven, because those heart-shaped chicken nuggets aren't fooling anybody.

When she's finished, Mrs. D tries to hand me the lunch slip, but I dig in my pocket and hand her a note back instead. Her eyes move back and forth over Mom's writing. "I guess you're on your own today," she says with a smile. She holds out the slip again, but I stick my hands behind my back.

"Actually, I was hoping Sofía could come with me anyway."

Mrs. D tilts her head at me. "Sure, if you want." She turns to Sofía and holds the slip out to her. At first Sofía doesn't move. She sits there looking kind of stunned. Finally, she gets up, takes the slip, and heads out of the room.

I follow her. But as soon as I get out the door, she whirls around to face me. Her flower headband is yellow today, and her eyes are shooting darts at me again. I swallow and wave for her to go first, but she just stands there with her mouth in a hard line until I tuck my chin and head down the hall.

She follows behind me while I walk to the first classroom. I slow down to let her catch up, but she hangs back even farther. Finally, when we get to the fifth-grade room, I nod at the slip on their door. "You can get it," I say.

She crosses her arms.

I shift to the other foot. "Really," I say. "Go ahead."

"Why? So you can yell at me again?" She

turns on her heel and marches down the hall.

This is going to be harder than I thought.

I take down the slip and hurry after her. When we get to fourth grade, I wave my hand at the door. "*Now* it's your turn," I say.

"I don't want a turn."

"Come on," I say, holding up my slip. "We're tied one to one. You can still win this thing!"

She rolls her eyes. But the rest of her doesn't budge. So finally I sigh and get the slip myself.

When I close the door behind me, she's already on the move. I start trailing her down the hall again, thinking like crazy. How am I going to get this girl some slips? "Look," I say as we pass the third-grade room, "I'm sorry I was mean to you yesterday."

Sofía responds with a *humph*.

"What? I'm trying to apologize here."

"It wasn't just yesterday."

I clench my fists. I feel the lava simmering, and I almost throw up my arms and yell, *What about you? What about what you did to me?*

But instead I grit my teeth so hard that my jaw starts to hurt. Luckily, that's when I remember to breathe. I suck in a big breath all the way down to my toes and let it leak out like I'm a balloon losing all its air.

Because fine. She's right, okay? She stopped

being my friend, but I stopped being hers right back. I didn't talk to her. I barely even looked at her. I looked at her clip instead.

When we get to the second-grade door, she turns and sticks her chin out at me.

I swallow down the rest of the lava as hard as I can. "Look," I say. I take another big breath and rush ahead before I chicken out. "I know you don't want to be friends anymore. I get it. There are a bunch of other things that matter to you more now. And even though that hurts my feelings, I still shouldn't be mean to you. I shouldn't keep trying to beat you either. And even if you don't want to be friends, that doesn't mean we have to be enemies, does it? That's all I'm saying."

I drop my eyes and wait for her to say something.

She doesn't.

I scratch the front of my neck and rock back on my heels. "That's it," I say. "Speech over."

The second-grade teacher must have seen us, because just then the door opens, and she swoops over and holds out a slip. I quickly look at Sofía then stick my hands in my pockets and take one giant step backward so Sofía has to take it.

I let out a breath. Finally! Now it's two to two!

When the door closes, Sofía keeps standing there, staring down at the slip in her hand. I watch her forehead wrinkle, and I'm not sure, but I think it might be a crack in her anger.

When she finally looks at me, her face is in full-on thinking mode, but it still feels like a long time before she asks, "Who says I don't want to be friends?"

I blink at her. "You did."

"I never said that."

"But—" I stutter. Because, okay, I guess she never actually said those words. "You stopped playing with me," I say. "That's the same thing."

"No, it isn't. You could have stayed in with me."

I scrunch up my nose. "Why would I do that?"

She stomps her foot. "Because you wanted to hang out with me!"

"To do extra work? Are you crazy?"

Her face is getting red, like maybe she's the one with lava inside her now. I actually take a step away because it looks like she's gonna blow.

I take a deep breath and start again. "What I mean is, if you want to get ahead in every single subject, that's up to you. I won't stop you." I swallow. "I was just mad because I missed you so much."

Sofía's eyes get wide. "I wasn't trying to get ahead. Is that what you thought?"

I don't know what to say to that, other than, "Well, yeah."

She tips her head back and squeezes her eyes

shut. When she finally talks, her voice is tight and shaky. "I don't stay in to get ahead," she says. "I stay in because I'm behind."

I am not expecting that. "What are you talking about?"

She groans and covers her face with her hands. "In math," she says. "I don't understand what we're doing half the time. It takes me forever to do the problems, and I still get tons of them wrong. Mrs. D has been giving me extra help and time to work during recess. That's why I stay in."

I can't believe my ears. "Why didn't you just tell me that?"

Sofía drops her hands and looks at me. Her lip starts to tremble, and the pain in her eyes is so bright that I almost have to look away. "You think I'm good at everything," she says. "How could I tell you I'm not?"

I stare at her. Then I pull myself up straight. I feel fierce—almost angry. This must be how the gazelle feels when she sees the lion coming for her friend. "Sofía María Rodríguez González." I use all her names so she knows I mean it. "You're talking to the girl who has never even once clipped to the top of the behavior chart. Why would I care if you're not good at everything?"

Her eyes are filling with tears.

"You're smart and nice and fun, and you like to

make stuff, and you've stuck with me since kinder-garten. *That's* what I care about."

She looks down at her feet and wipes her eyes with the back of her hand.

"I thought I wasn't good enough for you any-more," I say quietly.

"You're good enough," Sofía says. She gives me one of those teary smiles where the mouth turns down instead of up. "You're better than that."

But I don't feel better than that. I think about all those times she stayed in by herself when every-one else went out. I imagine her sitting alone at her desk, day after day, and my stomach starts to ache.

This is it, I realize: the Down I was wait-ing for. The one I wished would happen to Sofía instead of me.

I wanted something to hurt her. Only it turns out I already had.

Sofía takes a shuddery breath. Then she turns and starts walking to the first-grade room. This time, when I hurry after her, she slows down so I can walk beside her.

"Does it help?" I ask. "Staying in, I mean. Are you getting caught up?"

She sighs. "I'm doing okay with graphs, and I was starting to get the hang of multiplying." She shakes her head. "But I don't get dividing at all."

"It's the same as multiplying, only backward."

"You sound like Mrs. D. She says I just need to learn the fact families."

"Right," I say, nodding. "Once you know which numbers go together, you just need to make sure they stay that way." I scratch the back of my neck. "I could help you if you want."

Sofía gives me a weak smile. Then she hangs her head. "It probably won't make any difference. I'll never get it."

"Of course you will," I say, bumping my shoulder against hers. "You work harder than anybody. And you never give up on anything you care about." I swallow. "I should have remembered that about you."

She glances over and gives me the faintest smile before her eyebrows wrinkle again. "What about you?" she asks. "Are you okay? What's all this stuff about tumors and fireworks?"

I wave my hand. "I don't have a tumor," I say. "It's something way less serious." I slide my eyes over to her. "Maybe I can tell you about it at lunch."

"Maybe you can tell me at recess."

I stop at the door to the first-grade room. "Don't you have to stay in?"

"Mrs. D says I can go out whenever I want a day off." She bites her lip. "I just didn't think I had anybody to play with."

"Yes, you do," I say, bouncing on my toes. "Of *course* you do."

I reach into my back pocket, pull out a piece of paper, and try to hand it to her. She stares at it for a few seconds before she finally takes it. She has to unfold it about a million times, because the valentine I made her is as big as a treasure map.

For a while Sofía just stares at it. I look too, even though it's upside down to me.

I wrote her name in the most careful cursive letters I could. *S* is the swirliest, trickiest letter of all, but it's also the prettiest. I practiced and practiced

until I could make it beautiful, and I used every color in the world for the rest—the red oranges and the yellow greens and the blue violets. I even used black and white, because why shouldn't they have any fun?

But she doesn't look happy. She just stares at the valentine.

"What if I keep staying in?" she finally says. "What if I'm stuck doing catch-up work for the rest of my life?"

"Then I'll stay in with you. I'll work on handwriting, like you said. I don't care what we do. I just want to do it with you."

She looks up at me through her eyelashes. "Really?"

"Really." I hold out my pinky finger.

She smiles and hooks her pinky finger onto mine. With all the rubber bands on her teeth, it's the most colorful smile I've ever seen.

We stand there, hooked together and grinning. Then she tilts her head at me. "Your rainbows are brighter today," she says.

I give my hair a pat. "I touched it up this morning."

For just a second my heart twists inside me. I don't want to say what I'm thinking. But finally I blurt out, "Your heart hair was better."

Because come on. It was.

Sofía does a shy blink. "Thanks."

And just like that, I feel lighter, like I sent one of the last rocks inside my stomach skipping away, and it feels so good that I want to blurt out a bunch of other things, too.

"I'm sorry I kept trying to beat you at everything," I say. "And I'm sorry I made it seem like I didn't want to be friends. And I think your valentine box is the best one in the class."

My stomach is so light now, it might just whoosh up and fly away. I grab the knob and fling open the first-grade door.

Sofía walks into the classroom and steps up to the teacher. She looks over her shoulder at me. I give her a thumbs-up.

Then she takes the lunch slip. Her third.

When she comes back, I hold up my two slips—one in each hand—and grin.

"You win," I say.

I n the afternoon we take turns putting valentines in one another's boxes. Mrs. D lets me go first, because nothing will fit in my box until I open him up, take out all the beautiful trash, and put a bit of it into everyone's beautiful boxes.

I put the Easter grass in Eli's box to make it more nature-y. I give the red cheese wax to Pedro because it matches his scribbles. When I get to Sofía's flamingo, I dump in all the beads I found in the mud so we can make new brace-lets together. These will be stronger. This time I think they'll last. But even if they do break, we'll pick up the pieces and put them right back together again.

When I'm finished, I step back and take a long look at all our projects. Each one is so different from the others! Eli's is the woodiest. Pedro's is the messiest. Sofía's is definitely the prettiest. But I don't really know which box is the best. Maybe nobody's. Maybe everybody's.

Although mine *is* pretty great.

He looks fierce and colorful and proud of himself. There's no other box like him in the class. Maybe in the world. Before I go to my seat, I give him a little tap on the head. "Pleased to meet you," I whisper.

When I'm done, I watch the other kids give out their valentines. Whenever they get to mine and they have to open the egg carton and let their cards drop inside, everyone smiles. Some of them even giggle. That makes me feel happy all the way to my toes.

When we're all done, Mrs. D puts on some music. Maddy passes out cupcakes, Aiden gives everyone a juice box, and we carry our boxes back to our desks to read all our valentines. I open the trapdoor on mine and watch the little envelopes slide out the back.

I gasp. Because just like that, I get one more Inspiration.

I wasn't even planning on one of those!

I look around the pod of desks. "You guys," I say. Eli and Pedro and Sofía stop opening valentines and look at me. "Watch."

I feed an envelope back in through his teeth. I open the trapdoor and watch it slide out the back. I look back at everyone, kind of breathless.

"He poops valentines," I say.

Pedro yelps. Sofía covers her mouth. Eli leaps

up, slips a valentine into my box, then pulls the tab so it slides out again.

They're laughing now. And they all want a turn at feeding him. The next thing I know, everyone is crowding around my desk, feeding my box. And even though Mrs. D groans and shakes her head when she sees what we're doing, she just turns up the music, goes to the clip chart, and moves all our clothespins back to the start.

This is my kind of party!

I move out of the way so everybody can have a turn with my box.

But before I do, I grab the folded-up valentine that just slid out the back. I'd know that handwriting anywhere. It says my name in perfect cursive, in every color of the rainbow. I open it up and see Sofía's bar graph. It looks like colorful skyscrapers—high ones and low, red and pink and purple. Beneath them, I read something that's the best Up of all:

We've had our ups and downs, but I still want to be friends.

Can tabs are taped all over the page.

I look up. Sofía is smiling at me over the top of everybody's heads. I smile back. And I may not have rubber bands on my teeth, but it feels like my most colorful smile.

This is definitely one of my Ups. Right now. Right this minute.

I don't know what I'll have next, an Up or a Down.

But I'm Ready for Anything.

Acknowledgments

Thank you to the amazing team at Simon & Schuster Books for Young Readers who helped make this a better book! Thank you especially to my enthusiastic editor, Krista Vitola, and her assistant, Catherine Laudone. Heartfelt thanks also to Rayner Alencar for so beautifully capturing the spirit of this story and the characters who fill it.

I am grateful to Emily Mitchell of Wernick & Pratt Agency. You're a dream come true—professional, responsive, and funny. I'm so lucky to be working with you!

Thanks to everyone who offered feedback on early drafts: my family, critique groups (WritersInk and Sunday Writers), and Michele Simonson. Special thanks to Beth Pierce for reviewing my medical facts.

Of course, I am grateful to my family for always cheering me on. Most of all, I thank my husband, Brian Zanin. If I weren't bent on writing, we'd probably travel more and drink better wine, but ours is the only life I want. I'm grateful every day for it, and for you. Thank you, my love.

Author's Note

Meena's story, in many ways, is my daughter's story. One winter morning, when Amelia was nine years old, she woke up with a stomachache. We thought she was coming down with the flu until she had her first seizure. Although it only lasted for a minute, she was still unconscious when the paramedics arrived. She didn't have another seizure for months, although she did have spells of nausea that her neurologist referred to as "partial seizures." After an electroencephalogram (EEG) revealed abnormal electrical activity in her brain, Amelia was diagnosed with epilepsy and began taking anticonvulsant medication. For unknown reasons, her brain seemed to normalize later. Now a teenager, she has been seizure-free for years.

Not every child who has a seizure is epileptic. For instance, fever-induced seizures are fairly common in young children. For many people, however, epilepsy is a life-long condition. It may develop as the result of an illness or injury, but in most cases, no cause is ever found. The seizures themselves can vary greatly, depending on how and where they begin in the brain. The type that sends Meena to the hospital is called a generalized tonic-clonic or grand mal seizure. It involves loss of awareness and involuntary jerking, followed by a period of unconsciousness during which the brain "reboots." In other types of seizures, individuals may remain conscious. Seizures differ in length and severity. They may occur in the brain alone or cause movement in the body. Some have a known trigger, like flashing lights, while others occur without warning. Treatment plans also vary from one individual to the next.

Most people with epilepsy experience more than one type of seizure. Meena, for instance, has a tonic-clonic seizure as well as several absence seizures (her "spacing out"). She also experiences arm jerks in the morning, common to children with Juvenile Myoclonic Epilepsy. I know of one physician who refers to these as "cereal seizures" because they cause children to inadvertently fling cereal right off their spoons, as Meena does.

Meena also feels dizzy and nauseous before her tonic-clonic seizure. This sensation is called an aura. Some people experience light-headedness, blurred vision, a tingling sensation, or an unpleasant taste or smell before a seizure. Others feel a sudden intense emotion like fear or euphoria. Still others experience no aura whatsoever.

In my journey to learn more about my daughter's condition, I found the Epilepsy Foundation (https://www.epilepsy.com/) to be an invaluable resource. The online fact sheets from the Centers for Disease Control and the National Institute of Health are also a good starting point.

For the technically inclined: the *something* detected by Meena's CT (computed tomography or CAT) scan and necessitating further investigation with an MRI (magnetic resonance imaging) is called an arachnoid granulation. This is a common finding—basically a "bump" on the skull—that usually requires no intervention.

Dealing with a chronic condition can be scary for anyone. Like most children, however, Meena just wants to march on with her usual activities in the face of her symptoms. She is herself, not her diagnosis. Isn't that true for all of us? We have Ups and Downs. We deal with fear and uncertainty, whether because of a medical condition, a loss, or some other life change. Like Meena, we don't always get to choose what happens to us—only how we respond to it.

Life isn't perfect. It never will be.

But it can still be beautiful.